THE STRANGER

Supernatural Made Natural

Monique Payette

The Stranger
Copyright © 2022 Monique Payette

ISBN: 978-1-7782669-0-4

www.moniquepayette.com

DEDICATION

Dedicated to my loving father, Rene Gagnon who fought the cancer battle bravely thanking Jesus for every day and looking forward to his graduation day which occurred January 18, the exact day I finished writing this adventure, four years later.

ACKNOWLEDGEMENTS

Thank you to my Heavenly Father who breathed this idea and may this message glorify You.

Huge thanks to my mother who tracked my progress daily with her encouragement and my two sisters who believed in me.

So grateful to my husband and three children who inspired and cheered me on. Love you always.

Thank you to the wonderful editor, Fay's Book Editing who helped me every step of the way.

CONTENTS

CHAPTER ONE

September 24, 1999

It's 2:00 a.m., pitch black, and I'm awakened by strange moaning sounds coming from outside. I reluctantly grab my purple plush robe and gingerly tiptoe down the stairs to the front door. I pause to listen. Oh, there it is again! For land's sake, why does this have to happen when I'm all by myself? Well, a girl's got to be brave and face her fears, right? I quickly grab a flashlight from the junk drawer, quietly open the door a crack and peer out into the dark night, hoping it's just my ears playing tricks on me.

Nope, groaning emanates from a heap on my sidewalk. I rush over, forgetting my fears, wanting to help this poor soul. I point my flashlight with shaking fingers, trying to see through the bundled clothes, toque, and long brown hair poking out at weird angles.

It appears to be a man in his twenties holding his stomach where blood is seeping through his fingers. He's been stabbed! I hate the sight of blood, but I've seen enough movies to know you should apply pressure to stop the flow. In an instant, he flinches and passes out right before my eyes.

Panicking, I attempt to drag him inside to escape the cold and phone 911 to get some help ASAP. Being a French Canadian living on the farm and having to figure things out on my own, I quickly run through my options. The nearest hospital is a half-hour away and I cannot risk him losing too much blood. I could drive him myself, but I might make matters worse by moving him, so instead, I decide to call my pilot neighbor, Brian, to come to the rescue.

"Brian, sorry to wake you, but I have an emergency and I'm freaking out." I babble. "There's a wounded man on my doorstep, and the only way to save his life is to use your plane. Can you help me?"

"What?" He groggily replies. "Slow down Marina. Take a deep breath and tell me what you see."

"I think he's been knifed in the guts. He's losing a lot of blood. I'm applying pressure but he's passed out." I desperately reply. "Please come quickly. Time is of the essence!"

"OK, I will drive my truck over and be there as quickly as I can. Hold tight."

I'm thankful he's more than happy to oblige as he's always had a 'thing' for me, and for the time being, I'm willing to take advantage of that quality to aid this helpless man.

I can hear his diesel engine roaring down my lane, and I thank God for his quick response. Brian comes flying out the truck door and grasps the man under his arms. I grab his legs, and we carefully haul him into the back of the truck.

Brian has the foresight to grab an old sheet to rewrap the wound since it has seeped with all the jostling, while I support his head in my lap for the two-minute drive to the waiting plane.

Brian quickly helps me move him, and thankfully, our wounded stranger is still in and out of consciousness, delirious and not aware of his surroundings. I utter a quick plea upwards for a miracle to sustain this man who has somehow been plunked into my world out of nowhere.

What's taking Brian so long to get this plane rolling? I impatiently try to calm my rising desperation and bite my cheek to keep from screaming out, "We'd better get this bird in the air before I lose my cool!"

Thankfully, he appears in the doorway. "Plane check is complete," he says. "Are you both buckled and ready to go?" Yep, I was born ready, and tonight is the night to take action and help save this haggard stranger.

As the plane roars to life, I hope new life surges into his heart to keep it beating until we arrive to pass the baton on to the professionals. I have always loved flying and seeing things from a bird's eye view as it makes my life's problems seem so insignificant and part of a bigger plan. The quilt-like fields look like a mosaic, carefully planned out and designed.

The darkness is making its way to dawn, the first pinks are beginning to show in the cool cloud formations that never cease to amaze me, and I begin to feel hopeful that we will not be too late. God, will this be a day to celebrate or a day to grieve what I could've or should've done differently?

It's been eight minutes and I can finally see the small runway appear. I am grateful the rise and fall of the man's labored breathing can still be detected. On closer examination, I see that he has dark brown wavy hair that needs to be trimmed and a beard that's seen better groomed days, but the eyes that suddenly open in pain are the greenest I've ever seen at such close proximity.

I've never been kissed romantically by a man to date. Having lived for twenty-three years on this earth, I've never had the privilege of such close proximity before. But I digress. From the intense moment of reckoning that seems to be emanating from his sea-green eyes, "Where am I?" He asks groggily. "What is happening and why am I in so much pain?"

I am sure that is exactly what is going through his mind as I attempt to put him at ease.

"It's OK, sir. We are bringing you to the hospital, where they will get you fixed up in no time. Just you wait and see!" He receives that news and passes out again, which is just as well as he will be in a lot more pain shortly when we have to move him again.

As the plane bumpily shakes to a stop, I breathe a sigh of relief that help is on the way and I can pass the heavyweight of responsibility to the doctors and nurses. The part of the plan that I hadn't anticipated is how to get him from the airstrip to the hospital, but Brian's got me covered as he's already radioed in for an ambulance to be waiting.

The paramedics take over in true fashion, and I'm able to hop in as everybody knows each other in our small town. The girl on duty is my old high school friend Liz, who impishly quirks, "Hey, Marina, what did you get yourself involved in this time?"

I innocently shrug. "He just appeared on my sidewalk and I have no idea who he is or how he's been injured."

Liz takes in my blood-stained shirt and cautions me to stay out of the way as they hook him up to oxygen, check his vitals, and keep pressure on the wound. With sirens blaring, we pull into the ER where we're met by a stretcher and nurses who take in the critical situation and efficiently get him stabilized and rolling to the operating room.

As we race through the white corridors, I keep pleading with God to save him, as I don't believe his mission in life has been accomplished yet and the enemy is surely not going to snatch his life prematurely if I have any say in it. Of course, I have to stay behind closed doors and peek through the square window as they round the last corner into the operating room, leaving me declaring life into his body and the will to fight.

As the adrenaline begins to wear off, my legs begin to feel like jelly. I feel so lightheaded and drained. Brian appears right behind me, "I gotcha. Lean on me so you don't faint." He says. "Would you like some hot coffee and a cinnamon roll?"

"Thank you. You know that combo is my favorite. It will help pass the time as we wait to hear the outcome so we can get to the bottom of this mystery man," I reply.

Meanwhile, I have time to conjure up all sorts of scenarios of a jealous lover gone awry or a drug deal gone south, but what I really want is the truth and closure so I can resume my predictable life. This is as much excitement as I've seen in ages, and I just want sleep and normalcy to return to my rather boring and uncomplicated life.

I love living out in the country, surrounded by rolling farmland, grazing cows, farmers grousing about the weather, and the only worry being the price of wheat going down the tubes. I don't personally farm but I just enjoy renting out the land to my cousins and using the farm as a refuge to write novels, paint, and compose music, which I'd love to record one day.

Yes, I am one of those creative types that love to dream, but I do have a day job teaching piano and singing to some fifty-plus students at the local school. They affectionately call me their diva in training as I have never been on a date that has turned into a real relationship or what I refer to as someone I could imagine myself marrying. "Why date until you know you want to marry the guy?" is my motto!

So, I have many guy friends but no dating history to speak of. I'm perfectly happy with my life and I'm content. It may be lonely at times, but I'm not pining away waiting for Mr. Right to parachute his way into my life, thank you very much.

Ah, I can feel a headache coming on because of lack of sleep. I feel myself beginning to drift off with my head bobbing and jerking me awake every few minutes. Finally, Brian gently puts his arm around me and presses my head against his shoulder. My reddish, auburn curls tickle my cheek, and when my lashes finally close in sweet surrender, the nurse comes in with a clipboard to fill me in on our patient's status.

They've found his license and gathered that twenty-six-year-old Matteo Morales has apparently been knifed in the guts and has lost so much blood that he needs a blood transfusion.

"Do either of you happen to have O-negative blood?" The nurse asks hurriedly. "He needs a match pronto!"

I don't have the blood type to match, but Brian does, so he generously offers and leaves me by myself to be the hero once again.

I have a fleeting thought that my once safe little world is not so safe anymore. Who would knife someone around these parts anyway? This mystery man could spell trouble, and I don't need the extra drama in my cozy life. But who am I to not lend a helping hand to those in distress?

His name sounds Spanish, and his dark skin could lend credibility to that theory, but I should patiently wait to find out the true details and not jump to any foregone conclusions.

However, I love to spice things up, so I begin to envision a whole scene unrolling before my very eyes. My very hazel eyes love to see things through rose lenses and imagine all the different scenarios ahead of time and create my own foregone conclusions. I love my imaginative mind of endless possibilities, but I quickly sober to the fact that he's hurt and I should not profit from his pain.

Ah alas, the nurse is coming back with a worried look on her face. She asks me if I know that Brian has vasovagal syncope, which is a condition where a person faints when their body reacts to certain triggers, in this case, the sight of blood.

Oh dear, I feel as though I'm in a movie and this is not really happening. Poor Brian, this might wreak havoc on his macho pride, so I walk over to see if I can be of any help. I try not to chuckle, as I know that won't help the situation. Brian tends to exude confidence and likes being seen as a burly dude with an attitude and no weaknesses. This will not be good for his ego, so I won't rub it in, as that is not what good Christian girls do.

Brian is looking a little peaked with a chalk-white face, sweating bullets, and about to puke all over me. I quickly hand him the wastebasket, turn to give him privacy, and try not to gag as he empties his stomach painfully. This is not what I signed up for, but that's what friends are for, I guess, to support each other through thick and thin. Right now, it's thick and reeks!

My compassion finally kicks in long enough to get him a cool cloth and mop his perspiring brow, neck, and back, although that feels a little too intimate at the moment. He doesn't seem to care and just groans his appreciation, so I run to rinse the cloth and get it cool again to repeat the process until his sense of boundaries comes back and he declares that he is feeling better.

Meanwhile, Matteo is fighting for his life and is receiving the life-giving blood he needs to survive this whole terrible ordeal he remembers nothing about. Life sure has a way of throwing curveballs at you that makes you roll with the punches, so to speak. No pun intended, I'm just beyond tired. It's a good thing this kind of excitement doesn't happen every night, as my poor heart can't take it, I'm telling you.

When will they let me see him? I mean, I know I'm a stranger, but I am involved now. They're probably trying to locate his family and won't let me in, but I do have the advantage of living in the small coastal town of Hillersby, British Columbia, which boasts 8,000 people max. So, I know someone on the inside who can sneak me into his room so I can see his condition for myself.

Perfect, here comes Liz, the nurse, walking hurriedly towards me, beckoning me to come. I let Brian rest in his slouched position, while I half-run to keep up with long-legged Liz. My five-foot -four frame, weighing 132 pounds, matched with short, stocky farm girl legs, has to do double time, but I am only too happy to go see the state of Matteo for myself.

I enter his hospital room, thanking the good Lord it isn't the intensive care unit and grateful to see he's resting and breathing on his own, despite his white pallor from loss of blood. No tubes are hooked up to his mouth and only an IV is administering the fluids he so desperately needs. He is resting peacefully, so I decide to wait in the chair, and before I know it, I doze off, only to wake up and see him watching me with questions in his eyes.

I groggily sit up, as reality comes rushing back in full force, and stammer, "Oh hi, you're awake. That's great! How are you feeling after last night?"

He searches my face for any clues and responds huskily, "What happened and how do I know you?"

I hastily explain how I'd found him out in the cold and was wondering what had transpired before he collapsed on my sidewalk.

"I'm searching my mind for any clues and coming up empty. Sorry, it might come back to me bit by bit, I hope," he manages to croak out with an interesting accent.

Great, what I'd feared would happen, no closure and no direction to go from here. Well, the most important thing is not to stress him out but to allow his body to get healed, and maybe the details will come back slowly with time.

"I'll come back after supper to check on you. Please take care of yourself." I say as I prepare to take my leave.

He looks reluctant to be left alone, but I need to check on Brian and fly back to the farm to look after my kitties and get some beauty sleep.

Brian's just waking up from a nap and looks more like his ruddy self, ready to journey back home and tend to his chores too. We say our goodbyes to Liz, then Brian peeks in on Matteo to make sure he's indeed recovering, and we take our leave. Nothing remarkable happens on the way home, which is just as well. After a smooth landing, I give a quick side hug to Brian, slide into his truck, and look forward to being back in my home sweet home. At least I hope it is still sweet and innocent with no danger lurking about.

CHAPTER TWO

My calico mama cat, Daisy, welcomes me home, meowing her impatience that I'm late for her breakfast and lunch. I figure she's snacked on some mice while I was away, so she's probably not starving. I fill her bowl with cat food covered in tuna juice that I had saved and I'm rewarded with happy slurping sounds.

My dog, Bozer, yaps wildly, and I throw some leftovers in a dish for him and decide to take a leisurely soak in my clawfoot tub. Ah, c'est la belle vie! My candles, bubble bath, and Epsom salts are ready. Soft classical music fills the air, completing a perfect way to soak my sore muscles and stress away. Check and check. I decide to take the time to thank God for answering my prayers for protection. I pray that He will complete His healing touch on Matteo's body, soul, and mind.

Oh, I forgot to pray shock and trauma off Matteo when I was there. Oh well, after supper will not be too late, assuming he's even open to that sort of thing. There's only one way to find out, I'll ask his permission before I proceed.

As I towel dry my naturally curly hair, I decide to check in on the five-week-old kitties that Daisy is busy feeding and make sure none are in danger of being squished into a pancake. Life on the farm can be so cruel at times. I also have to make sure the tomcat isn't around as he would still try to kill the male kittens for less competition down the road. Ah, males and their turf! All is peaceful, so I quickly make an egg sandwich in the microwave for lunch and serve it with some cranberry juice. After lunch, I retire for a much-needed nap on the sunny couch, much like a cat myself basking in the sunshine.

I wake to a scratching noise by the window but think nothing of it as Bozer usually alerts me to any danger, so I yawn, roll over and keep napping, knowing that a fifteen-minute nap will not sustain me this time.

The phone ringing gets me up as I want to make sure it isn't the hospital trying to get ahold of me. Nope, it's probably just some marketer trying to upsell me on some type of bundle. Not today, I'm not in the mood. My body feels like it's been run over by a truck.

It's time to make a shake, pack some homemade buns and soup to bring to my new patient, and hit the road with my red Honda Civic. I absolutely adore it. It's peppy, great on fuel, and easy to park, which is just my kind of ride. I decide to text Brian and offer him a ride, but he has fieldwork to do and haying cannot wait as the rain clouds are threatening to roll in.

The relaxing drive through the fall colors has a way of making me want to sing. It reminds me of all the blessings I have in my life that I should be thankful for. I have good health, family, friends, and a really good life that I love to live to the fullest! Isn't that why we were created, to glorify God, enjoy Him in all that we do, and live a life worthy of His pleasure?

Oh no, I suddenly slam on the brakes trying not to fishtail as I see a moose in the ditch about to cross. Even though I can't wait to see Jesus face to face, I know this is not my time to graduate just yet. I haven't fulfilled my life's mission on earth. How do I know that? I can feel it in my bones and just have an inner knowing. As I slow down to watch the moose cross the highway, I am struck by the majesty of this magnificent animal, and this particular male has a huge rack on him! Mesmerizing! I know my cousin would love to bag it for his freezer and because it is hunting season, I might just have to keep quiet about my sighting this time. Wink wink.

As I round the last corner and enter the hospital doors laden with my goodies, I notice a gloomy atmosphere or heaviness in the air. I dismiss all evil under my breath and release God's anointing to bring His life and joy into the place. I firmly believe that as we walk in life, we can change the spiritual atmosphere of a place and clear the air of any evil that the dark side is trying to dictate. We are all called to take dominion on this earth as it is in heaven, so we might as well exercise our God-given authority! I sense a change already, as I greet people with a smile and an encouraging nod. Life is a gift and every breath is precious, as many people in this place know firsthand. To say the least, Matteo right at this moment is struggling to cling to life.

Wow, I sense angels in his room, and sure enough, his coloring is looking a whole lot better than the green white I was used to seeing. I see the nurses had a chance to give him a close shave and trim his locks, which makes him appear, dare I say, handsome and less vagabond-like. His attention is riveted to the news, where an announcer is claiming that a woman's body had been found washed ashore and asking if anyone could identify her or possessed firsthand knowledge to please come forward. Matteo's countenance has once again turned ashen, so I figure he might be privy to some inside information. Interesting...

I flounce into the room with my homemade buns wafting a heavenly aroma and my creamy cheesy chicken chowder (I might just share the recipe with you in appendix A) smelling divine and I deposit the bounty on his side table. All the while, I maintain eye contact to see if he might spill the beans on what he knows.

He guardedly welcomes me with a hesitant smile and accepts my offering with simple gratitude. This is fine since we are virtually strangers and still haven't had a full-on conversation to speak of. Ha, there I go sounding all punny again.

At least he takes the time to breathe in the mouthwatering goodness, and I am satisfied that my food is appreciated as he spoons in the first bite and sighs appropriately. #1 mission accomplished, and #2 is still to pray shock and trauma off of this poor, injured man who must've been at the wrong place at the wrong time.

I politely ask if I can pray with him, and he shrugs that he doesn't mind. He even puts his spoon down and closes his eyes. Hmpf, he must know something about God, I deduce. I gingerly put a hand on his shoulder and start praying, "Lord Jesus, we thank you for your son. Thank you for saving his life. I dismiss all the shock and trauma from the accident in his mind, body, will, and emotions. I release the negative effects from his soul and bless his body to heal with no infections in Jesus' Name."

"Amen." He seems to receive the prayer as he breathes out a big sigh and resumes biting into the soft bun.

Then he decides to speak at last, "Why are you doing this for me, being so nice? What is your name?"

Good questions. What are my motives?

"Well, I was taught to be a Good Samaritan and would want the same kindness shown to me. I'm also invested now and I want to see you restored and connected back to your life again. Oh, and my name is Marina."

He tries to say my name with the French accent I used and succeeds pretty well. "Thank you, Marina. Could you please do me a favor and get a message to my aunt that I am OK?" He asks. When I nod, he hands me a card, "Here's her number."

I try not to react when I notice that the area code is not from British Columbia but from Africa, where there is war and civil unrest, which means he has no one nearby to lean on. Brian might need to come to the rescue again! I do the mental math of the time difference and note that it is now 2:00 a.m. there. "Isn't it too late to put a call across?" I ask. "We might wake her."

He replies, "No, she will be very worried and she's probably praying for me right now anyway."

Ah, so he is used to being around people of faith in God. Good to know.

I decide to go find a secluded spot where I can have some privacy and dial the number. Holding my breath nervously, I'm trying to think of a way to explain without causing her panic when I hear a relieved voice saying, "Oh thank you, Jesus! I am finally going to get some answers as to why my nephew is M.I.A. and not responding to my texts."

I introduce myself and explain that he is stable and recovering in a hospital from a knife wound. "I knew he was in trouble as the Lord put it on my heart to pray and fast all night." She exclaims. "Where is he? Can I speak to him? Does he remember what happened?"

I respond by filling her in on his whereabouts. "He's resting and hasn't spoken to anyone yet about the incident."

Unbeknownst to me, the police and reporters have converged on his room and are trying to pry any information they can out of him. Matteo is playing it calmly and not divulging any pertinent details, as he hasn't yet pieced everything together. He feigns their onslaught and manages to dissuade them for the time being, hoping for some solitude to formulate his own conclusions. He is also hoping his aunt, Mindy, will stay put in Africa and not try to be his Florence Nightingale.

Meanwhile, Mindy is definitely gearing up to come to nurse him back to full health so he can fulfill his mastermind invention that has high-profile people all over the world trying to get their hands on it before he goes public. No wonder he was stabbed! He needs protection, an escort, and some heavenly interference to help see this project through to the end, and she is just the woman to fulfill that mission.

At this point, Marina has no clue as to the seriousness of the situation or what is going on behind the scenes. She will also need protection. Aunt Mindy decides she can do both! She books her ticket quickly. They do not even need to know she's going to be on their radar very soon. They can deal with her once she lands. All she needs is to get a house sitter for the month she will be away, pack a small bag, and plan her veto on the long plane ride.

Marina is surprised that his aunt is so amicable about the whole ordeal. She returns to Matteo's side to fill him in on the good news, only to find him fast asleep. Ah, just as well; he needs to recover so they can get to the bottom of this mystery.

CHAPTER THREE

I find myself asking what my dad would do in this situation. He passed away from colon cancer three years ago, and I still miss his advice, prayers, and listening ears. I can still smell his mouth-watering breakfasts of sizzling crispy bacon, eggs fried to perfection, strong coffee, and homemade bread toasted with butter. I wonder why I'm feeling famished all of a sudden but I ignore my growling stomach and try to reach out to my family.

I have a loving family. My mom is my biggest cheerleader and my two older sisters are my confidantes, but they live a province or two away. So, that leaves Brian, Liz, my cousins, and my soul sisters, whom I see every other week at bible study, to help come up with a tactical plan. I know my family has me covered in prayers. I just need to let them know what's going on, as I haven't had a chance to share any of this craziness! There's no better way than to connect with a four-way call.

The call is met with shrieks and exclamations, "Are you OK?" "Don't put yourself in harm's way," "Maybe you should just leave it to Brian to figure out" and "God must have a plan since he was dumped on your doorstep."

You see, our French family loves to talk all at the same time, gesture wildly, and put our two cents in, and yet we all understand each other perfectly. We're not being rude by interrupting because this is how we've always communicated. I, however, did have to learn to take turns speaking in the English world so as not to appear too rude. I think it takes the fun out of communicating as I have to damper my enthusiasm, but a girl needs to keep her friends, right? After an hour of hashing out ideas, I reluctantly say my goodbyes and promise to keep them updated.

I hear someone pulling into the yard, and it sounds like a diesel engine to my trained ear. Interestingly, my dad, Pete, taught me about all things mechanical. He was a heavy-duty mechanic in the oilfield and I got to work on engines that, to my eight-year-old mind, seemed to be the size of a house.

I mostly washed parts in paint thinner, handed him tools, and learned the vocabulary of how to check and clean the spark plugs. I loved spending time watching him do what he knew best. He made sure I stayed clear when things didn't go his way, as tools might start to get airborne and choice words could be heard.

I look out the window and see Brian, wrapped in his blue flannel lumberjack shirt, looking tired as he probably worked in the fields all night long. It was nice of him to check in on me with his busy schedule. He looks worriedly up at the grey clouds blowing in and rushes to my front porch to knock, but I beat him to it by opening the door with a flourish.

"Brian, good to see you. It looks like you've been busy." I hand him a cup of hot coffee to warm his hands. "Come on in and take a load off."

He nods appreciatively and takes a seat at my antique farm table, asking about Matteo's condition. I fill him in on all the happenings while making my own version of Dad's breakfast to tide us over for the busy day ahead. We discuss the possible scenarios linked to the stabbing and both haven't heard any rumors surrounding it other than what was broadcast on the news blasting that morning: "A dead body was found ashore at 5:00 a.m. by some local fishermen. Please come forward with any information."

"Oh Lord, this is getting more mysterious with every passing day. What is happening to our sleepy town?" I wonder aloud.

"Maybe if we take the time to drive into town and hobnob at the Old Grind coffee shop, we might be rewarded with some juicy gossip that could give us some clues." Brian holds the hot coffee cup close. "Or perhaps just lead us down another bunny trail... but it's worth a shot."

"Or we can ask for wisdom and discernment and get the inside track with a little help from God," I quickly suggest.

Brian agrees that prayer never hurts, and so we hold hands and ask God to guide us and bring the right people to help us in our quest for truth. After a delicious breakfast that leaves us both satisfied, we head our separate ways to do some sleuthing.

I decide to lay low for the time being to gear up for my week of teaching, prepare the music for church tomorrow, and hopefully meet with my soul sisters to get this off of my chest before I explode. They might've heard of some news or have some ideas as to how we should move forward in our private investigation for Matteo's sake.

I feel a sudden urge to drive to the beach, ten minutes away, to see if there are any clues left behind, but also to clear my head with the briny sea breeze and drink in the beauty of the waves crashing in on their own rhythmic cadence. How I love the ocean! It so refreshes me! I think it's something about the glory of God that hovers over the waters, so my mom, Gloria, taught me from the Word. It's true, His creation beckons and speaks to all who are open to recognizing it. I am always chasing the next sunrise and sunset pictures, trying to capture the beauty on camera as the colors speak to my soul.

Good thing I packed an extra sweater as it's cooler with the wind chill and I am excited that it's low tide so I can find sea treasures or clues. I park at the end of the cove where there are rocks, caves, crevices, and tidal pools to explore. I never tire of sticking my toes in the green sea anemones and watching them retract their sticky tentacles and then come back out when it's safe. I get sidetracked by flipping rocks and spying the baby crabs of various colors scrambling for cover; white, brown, black, green, or mottled camouflage. I breathe in the tangy smell of rotting seaweed and detect a campfire as well as music coming from down the beach.

OK, down to business. I spot a red object poking out from under a rock in the sand and, on closer examination, see that it's a leather wallet. Oh boy, this is evidence and I should just turn it in to the local authorities, but who says I can't sneak a peek? Then, I can tell Matteo pronto, and together we can deduce our own conclusions.

As I peel open the wet cover, I notice the soggy dollar bills and business cards and search for her license, assuming it's from the recovered woman from the news. The laminated license is protected by the plastic sleeve and shows the unsmiling face of a thirty-eight-year-old, Sarena Sanchez, a Caucasian female from Casey, Illinois. I wonder what brought her to my town; she is far from home! I think it is time to see if Matteo knows anything about this town or this woman. Off to Hillersby I go.

As I jump into my Civic that still has half a tank of gas, I contemplate if I should let Brian know what I've found but decide to play this out with Matteo first. I try to think like a detective, so I take pictures with my cell phone of the wallet and its contents. I have a twenty-minute drive to get to the hospital but notice a white truck starting to speed up behind me that seems to want to chase me down!

What is this guy's problem, and where did he come from? I notice he is wearing a cowboy hat and has a black beard, and as I speed up to see if I'm imagining things, he starts swerving and is right on my tail. I know these roads like the back of my hand, so at the last second, I turn left onto a gravel road, but he manages to skid around the corner and keeps following in my dust cloud. I wonder if he saw me at the beach and was spying on me. The nerve! I know this road merges back onto the highway in five kilometers, so I step on it and try not to lose control on the loose gravel. I send a panicked plea upwards, hoping for some divine intervention. I need a little help down here!

His truck is managing to keep up, so I decide to speed up to 110 kilometers an hour hoping he has less experience and will start to swerve because of the loose gravel and potholes. My Honda Civic knows how to dodge these potholes efficiently, and I am gaining ground. I'm trying to see his license plate so I can report him or see if it will jog Matteo's memory at all. But my big dust cloud makes it impossible at the moment, and I am forced to focus on the road so I don't land up in the ditch despite my best efforts at staying alive.

Phew, I see the last curve up ahead before the stop sign, and I know there's a little trail to the right, heavily populated with trees. I escape detection and hide out while he continues straight to town, thinking he's still chasing me down. He can't be smart enough to even think he lost sight of me at the last bend in the road. I doubt he's from these parts, but I make sure I am perfectly hidden. I take the time to collect my racing thoughts, as I breathe deeply to calm my beating heart and rethink my part in this whole ordeal.

I am not safe on my own anymore, so I either have to bring Bozer along as protection or one other person, and I don't want to cause trouble for my students or friends. What day is it anyhow? I've lost all track of time but I'm guessing it's Saturday, which means I have church tomorrow and I go back to reality on Monday. It's a good thing I only have to play the piano and sing, as I am in no shape to be leading others into worship. I just need to be still, ask for peace in this turmoil, and focus on Him who can calm every storm.

OK, it's time to get a move on. I think the crazy driver should be long gone and I can safely get to the hospital to deliver my auspicious findings. As I slink forward, ever watchful of the road, I'm relieved to see more traffic, so I slowly make my way onto the highway and decide to take a roundabout route to the hospital just in case. No sense leading him right to my patient, and plus, I need more time to think this thing through.

I text Liz, knowing she's on duty to meet me at the side door where the nurses have access and to get me in the back way to avoid any confrontations. She knows me well enough to not even ask questions and can come through for me. What a gem! I promise to fill her in on the details later at our soul sister's meeting the next evening.

I protectively hide my bag, with the wallet hidden in it, behind my back and hurriedly walk into his room, only to find a woman in her forties, wearing a bright floral wraparound dress, sitting next to him. She is talking animatedly and almost knocks me out with her wide arm gestures when she finally notices me.

"Oh, you must be the guardian angel who rescued my Matty from dying in a pool of his own blood that dark night. Come here, dear, so I can give you a proper hug and thank you from the bottom of my heart."

Man, I thought I was expressive with my French mannerisms. Nope, she's got me beat! This force of nature must be Aunt Mindy, who flew all night to get to her nephew in record time. "My, you made record time to get here." I return her warm embrace. "You two must be very close."

Matteo is looking a little peaked and smiles as he introduces me to his aunt, who exclaims what a godsend I am, while I assure her that he landed on my doorstep and anyone would have done the same around here.

"Well, I think organizing the plane was quick thinking and God had His hand in this all along, I'm telling you," she emphasizes by punching the air to prove her point.

I nod, all the while noticing they've been scheming as she takes the time to put a notebook away in her purse. I decide I should trust her and share with both of them my initial find at the seashore. They both jump when I show them the red wallet, as recognition dawns when they read the woman's name, then react sadly as they realize she was the drowned victim found on the news.

Hmm, she must've been an ally, and Matteo must not have been involved in her murder. So, I go on to tell them about the driver of the white truck that was tailgating me and describe his features. They exchange worried glances and stare at the corridor as if expecting him to appear before their very eyes. So, he must be the enemy, wanting information bad enough to kill for it. We will need vigilance and bodyguards around the clock. Should we involve the police? We can't be sure which side they are on.

As we discuss the specifics, I see they're choosing to trust me too, which is just as well. There is no going back now. Security is an issue, so I suggest that once they release Matteo to recuperate at home, they could either stay at my house or Brian's or someone from the church, but they are reluctant to draw any of us into the direct line of fire.

Mindy wants to stay by Matteo's side for the night, and I invite her to stay at my house when she is ready to leave his side. I try not to ask too many questions as to why Matteo is in such high demand to bring in this kind of attention. I can see he needs to rest to regain his strength. My queries and curiosity will have to wait another day. This sleuthing business is hard on the nerves. I need some chamomile tea and some comfort food. Maybe a scone will do the trick.

Feeling refreshed after eating, I decide to call an earlier soul sister meeting so I can hit the hay at a decent time to be ready for music on Sunday. They are eager to comply as we're having a potluck, which means I'd better make my famous barbecue ribs and pumpkin cheesecake for dessert. I also decide that the fall weather calls for some cinnamon-spiced hot apple cider and a warm fireplace to snuggle by.

I must check on my kittens too and feed all of my pets, including my fighter fish, Marvelous. Bozer is more than happy to greet me with his hello yips and slurpy kisses and he runs around me in circles. Gosh, you'd think I was gone for a month with that reception. My dog has taught me a lot about unconditional love. He is always joyful, never grumpy, and ready to seize the day!

I start on my dessert, light the BBQ, change into my comfy joggers and knit sweater, and put on some music. I try not to think about the cowboy guy on the loose and lock my door just in case, until the girls arrive on the scene. I take the time to pet the kitties as they de-stress me and I journal a few pertinent details so I don't forget anything from the last thirty-six hours.

I can attest to the divine smell permeating the air as five out of the seven ladies come trailing in with their dishes of yumminess. We are going to feast tonight! After all the hugs and promises to catch up over supper, we prepare the table to partake. We say a heartfelt thanksgiving prayer to God for the bounty, friendships, and His protection. Amidst sweet corn on the cob, potato salad, pickled carrots, pecan green beans, roasted avocado, ribs, and punch, the cacophony of six females all talking about their week fills the air.

All of a sudden, they stop in unison and look at me expectantly, wanting to hear about my week, as all they've heard thus far is that I had news and called them in early for a reason. I tell them everything starting from the night I found Matteo, to the plane ride, the drowned woman, finding her wallet at the beach, the car chase, Aunt Mindy, and not knowing who I could trust in the police department. We all know what greed, power, and money can do to change a good person.

They concur that we should pray and ask for wisdom, but first, they have a whole lot of questions that I have no answers to and show concern for my safety. I jot down some of their ideas of who to approach, which questions I should focus on (like getting more info out of Matteo), and what our tactical plan will be. They promise to, in turn, listen for any news in town, and take turns having sleepovers to make sure I am not alone. They also plan to map out all the known details on my office wall with sticky notes of all colors, just like a regular crime scene investigation in the movies.

But, first things first, it's dessert time. After dessert, we go for a soak in the hot tub and relaxing girl talk time. They are always trying to set me up with Brian, but now they are asking pointed questions about whether Matteo is dark and handsome too. Maybe God parachuted him right down on my sidewalk as fate.

As the stars come out, the girls realize it's time to leave and let me get my beauty sleep for church tomorrow. With leftovers in hand, hugs all around, and promises to see each other in the morning, my house is quiet once again and I am left to my own twirling thoughts that need to calm down so I can rest.

Oh, Linda, one of my soul sisters, who also teaches at the school is back on my stoop offering to sleep the night, so I am not alone, and I gladly take her up on it as I recall that scratching noise from the other day. I let her borrow some PJs and a new toothbrush, and make sure the guest room is up to snuff. We set our alarms for 7:00 a.m. as she is also singing with me at church.

CHAPTER FOUR

Suddenly, we wake up to hear Bozer barking uproariously, enough to wake the dead! My eyes search for the time. It's only 3:03 a.m., which has me groaning in frustration that my beauty sleep has been disrupted once again. I stumble around in the dark trying to find my robe and stub my toe on the corner of my dresser, eliciting a howl of agony. I hop on one foot for a while and as the pain eases, I rush downstairs in search of my flashlight. Bingo! I found it on my shelf on the porch. I throw my rubber boots on and then point the beam of light around, hoping to see what the commotion is all about.

All I hear is an owl hooting and the wind blowing through the trees, but I can't see anything out of the ordinary. I'm tempted to follow the sound of Bozer's yapping, which will lead me in the right direction, but I wisely wait for Linda to catch up.

"Oh my, why do we need to have this much excitement on a night when we both have to be up early?" Linda moans.

"I know, none of this is ideal, but we should investigate to see if we can find any clues to help solve this case for Matteo's sake," I whisper.

"OK, I will stay close behind you and be your backup," rejoins Linda.

The barking leads us to the trail behind the garage leading into the forest where Bozer is sniffing the ground. I try to hush him so as not to alert the enemy, but short of a muzzle, he is having none of it. I notice boot prints on the muddy trail as it had drizzled during the night and they are leading towards my house. Shucks, the person may have doubled back and could be in the house for all I know! I grab a stick and head back running, hoping we're not too late to get some answers.

"Please be careful," Linda yells at my retreating back. "Maybe we should call Brian and wait before charging into the house. What if it's a trap?" I know time is ticking away, so I run to the side door that rarely gets used, but it won't budge. The back door is locked as well, so that means that I have to go in through the front, where we came dashing out.

My heart is pumping with adrenaline, so I try to steady my breathing to be as stealthy as I can. I tiptoe up the porch steps, expertly avoiding the creaky spots. I gingerly open the screen door, holding my stick like a bat, and peer into the dark house. I pause to listen for any strange noises but I don't hear or see anything out of place.

Maybe I'm imagining all of this and this scare is for nothing, but I can usually trust Bozer's instincts. The memory of the white truck chasing me is enough to spur me onwards, and I keep walking with Linda and Bozer behind me, giving me support.

I've trained my dog with hand signals to know when to be silent, and at the moment he's being cooperative, which helps our stealth mission. As we tiptoe into the dark house, which I can navigate with my eyes closed, I ask for protection and believe that our guardian angels are working overtime tonight.

The kitchen is clear. There is no sign of any movement in the living room, and the hallway to the bathroom is empty. We split up so I can check the upstairs bedrooms while Linda checks the basement with a flashlight that I always keep at the top of the stairs on a shelf for emergencies. I've stationed Bozer at the front door to alert me if the intruder tries to escape. I quickly scan each bedroom, looking behind the doors. I don't see anything amiss except I don't remember leaving my desk drawer half-open in my office.

We re-group on the main floor, where Linda reports, "I didn't see or hear anything. We're all clear."

I sigh with relief, and we both decide to call it quits for now and go back to bed to salvage a few more hours of much-needed sleep. I decide to take melatonin as I feel too worked up with zillions of thoughts racing through my head. I surrender my worries to God and ask for His shalom peace to quiet my mind. I also pray to replace all the anxiety, shock, and trauma in my soul with His life, love, and grace.

I awaken to my alarm music and groggily stumble into the shower to wash away all the cobwebs while remembering that last night was not a dream. Wow, I need to start journaling about all of this when I get the chance, maybe tonight.

I can hear Linda rummaging around, so I decide to brew a fresh pot of Nabob dark roast coffee to give us a caffeine boost to energize us for our day. Then I feed my pets, who are begging for food with their pleading eyes. I fry up some local fresh farm eggs with kale, mushrooms, peppers, feta, green onions, and sesame oil. Nothing beats fresh farm produce from my garden to brighten our palates, yum!

Linda looks all spiffy in her green jumper as it sets off her green eyes and red hair quite nicely. She readily accepts the coffee and breakfast and exclaims that last night was quite an epic adventure.

"Did you notice any clues this morning in the light of day?" She queries.

"Not much, just a slightly open desk drawer and an unlocked back door. I assume we did not imagine the whole episode last night and our suspect was looking for information but escaped out the back door."

"How did he sneak right by us and not alert Bozer? At least he didn't try to harm us, but who knows if he'll get desperate enough because he can't find whatever he's looking for." She takes a sip of her coffee. "We might need to involve the police because this is getting out of our control. What does he think you have?"

I was pondering the same thing, and I agree that I might need to confide in Liam, my police officer friend, whom I trust and will see at church but not anybody else at the station for now. Baby steps are prudent to move forward.

"Let's get a move on so we're not late for practice. Thanks so much for staying with me, Linda. I would've felt a lot more vulnerable last night if I was alone, but you gave me the courage to face the enemy head-on." We get up to leave. "We'll see which soul sister will be brave enough to join me tonight once word of this gets out to our group," I say as we walk out the door.

At this point, I don't really want to involve more family or cousins so as not to endanger them. The less they know, the better. I figure I have enough support with my soul sisters, immediate family, Brian, Mindy, and now Liam, hopefully.

The church is packed. Most of the 250 seats are taken as people have heard the news and gathered to support and rally together. People respond to the music with exuberance and full-throated singing, giving praise to God in the midst of uncertainty. We can feel His abiding presence, bringing peace to our souls.

Pastor Ted shares from his heart how to persevere through trials and how that produces endurance, which refines our character and leads us back to hope (Rom 5:3-4). Well, I guess my character is being refined. I'm learning how to endure these new trials in my life, so that gives me hope!

I hurry to find Liam after the service. I ask for his help and set up a time for us to meet later. He seems curious, but he chooses to wait and does not ask any probing questions, which I appreciate.

Then, I corner the soul sisters and ask, "Who is brave enough to sleep at my house tonight? We never know what's going to happen next in this real-life mystery that we're all kind of involved in now."

Susie offers as she is a single, twenty-two-year-old veterinary technician, which provides her with a flexible schedule to accommodate me in my new craziness. I thank her for her willingness to help me out, and she tells me that she plans on joining me after supper.

I bump into Brian going out to my car and he wants an update, which I promise I'll give him later after I visit Matteo and Mindy to see where they're at in their findings. He reluctantly lets me go as he's made lunch plans but looks concerned for me as I race off to the hospital.

I decide to pick up some sushi on the way to share as I am feeling rather famished. As I'm leaving the grocery store, I glimpse the cowboy hat dude from the chase coming into the store. I try not to stand out as much as I can. As soon as I get to the parking lot, I scan for his white truck, hoping to memorize his license plates.

Hidden in the corner by some trees, I notice a similar truck so I quickly take a picture with my cell phone as I drive by. Excited with this new information, I quickly send the picture to Liam to see if he can uncover any details as to the identity of this stranger to town.

Now, he's really going to want to meet with me pronto as he must suspect I know something about what's been happening. Obviously, the police kept him in the dark about Matteo being found on my stoop. I know he would've called me ASAP to make sure I was OK.

Things are happening quickly, and I mourn my usual quiet time that

I get to enjoy on Sundays and promise myself that this will all be over soon and I can return to my content, peaceful life on the farm.

Arriving at the hospital in record time, I spot Mindy heading to the cafeteria, and I hurry to intersect her path to show her our treat so she can pass on the blah hospital food.

"Oh good, you are a godsend. I am so ready to eat healthier food and Matteo loves sushi." She smiles. "This will brighten his day too!"

"How are you guys holding up? Are the doctors talking about releasing him soon?" I ask.

"There is no infection and the wound is healing nicely. So, they may discharge him tomorrow, but the police don't want him to leave town yet."

"Great, I can see if Brian will let him stay at his house, or you can both stay at my house if you like."

Mindy seems to mull this over and thinks that my house might be a good option if it's not too much of an imposition. I assure her that I have the space, but wherever they feel more comfortable recuperating is fine with me. This arrangement will also let Susie off the hook, for now, so she doesn't have to rearrange her life for me. I send her a quick text to let her know, and she assures me she can help out anytime if I still need her later on. True friends of the heart are such a blessing to have.

Matteo seems more hesitant and does not want to be a burden, but I assure him that we have a lot to figure out and it'll be easier to have him in close proximity. I didn't tell him this but his puppy dog look is beginning to grow on me.

We devour the sushi with relish. I love how the wasabi and ginger flavors burst in my mouth, awakening my taste buds. I don't really like the burn of the nostrils, but it's a part of the experience as a whole. I usually make my own California rolls, but time is not much of a commodity these days. I feel like I am running on fumes and I look forward to an undisturbed full night's sleep. A soak in the hot tub sounds heavenly right about now. My bones feel achy and my feet and hands are always so cold.

Before I take my leave, I ask Matteo if I can have the red wallet back to show my friend Liam, who might help us on the case. He is reluctant to trust anyone new and assures me it is in a safe place for now. He doesn't want to endanger me further with the cowboy hat guy rooting around. I recall the photos I'd taken of the wallet, so I can start with that and do my own research on Sarena Sanchez.

I suddenly recall the picture I took of the white truck's plates, so I show it to them and they both show doubly worried expressions. OK, 'stay away from that dude' is the message I'm getting loud and clear. I will question them further about it on my own turf tomorrow away from prying eyes and ears.

I ask if we can pray together to ask for wisdom, discernment, and protection before I leave. Mindy is pleased as punch and Matteo nods gratefully, knowing we need all the help we can get. Mindy prays, "Lord, we feel as if we are out of control, in over our heads. We surrender all of our preconceived ideas into Your capable hands. You know where we should focus our attention and we ask for Your plan to prepare the way before us. Please send the right people into our paths to aid us in protecting and patenting the invention you've given to Matteo for such a time as this. In Jesus' Name, we pray."

"Amen," We chorus.

"I can't wait to hear about this brilliant invention of yours, Matteo, that people are willing to die for to get for themselves," I exclaim.

Matteo nods patiently with a gleam in his sea-green eyes and I furtively look around to see if there are any nosy doctors or nurses within earshot. No, all good, whew!

As I drive home, I check my rearview mirror to make sure I am indeed alone. I ponder all of the implications, people involved, and what part God has for me to play in this whole shemozzle! He must have a good reason and I'm glad He's in control and I'm not!

All seems well on the home front, so I select my burnt orange bikini, grab some lemon water, and sigh with relief as the outdoor hot tub embraces my chilled body. I sink into the deepest seat where the hardest jets pound out the stress from my lower back in a steady rhythm. Ah, this is the life! My dad would've loved to join me if he was still alive, but he might be peeking from his heavenly portal even now praying for me. He loved to soak for hours in my hot tub, and we'd have the best conversations ever. He also had a few good inventions up his sleeve, and maybe I should revisit those and join in on the creative inventing going on. I'm already busy composing songs for a CD, but it might be fun to do something with my mom and sisters in honor of my father.

Oh, shoot, I forgot that Liam is scheduled to come over at any time. I have no idea what the actual time is but I'm guessing I still have a few minutes to relax. I'm looking forward to seeing what new information he comes up with from the plates of the white truck. I will also show him the pictures I took of the red wallet. Between all of us, we should be able to come up with some concrete conclusions.

I hear his diesel engine rumbling down the side road and know my soaking time is up. He spots me with his trained cop eyes, and I signal that I will meet him momentarily after I change into something more suitable.

Liam is playing fetch with Bozer in the yard by the time I come down in my comfies, which consist of camo sweats and a black hoodie.

"Hey Marina, you've got a lot to bring me up to date on. What have you gotten yourself involved in this time?"

We're good enough friends to skip the pleasantries and get right down to business, so I explain from the beginning about a hurt stranger that landed on my farm in the middle of the night. As I progress through the details, he begins jotting notes down while tracking along with me.

I invite him inside for some coffee and lemon scones that Brian probably dropped off while I was in town. How thoughtful of him. Liam begins a search for information on Sarena Sanchez on his personal laptop from the pictures I took. He is worried about whom to trust in the department, so he is keeping it on the down-low for now.

Oh, interesting. Sarena is from Casey, a town that specializes in fourteen Guinness World Records for the largest structures made of recycled materials such as a wind chime, rocking chair, mailbox, pitchfork, teeter-totter, knitting needles, crochet hook, yardstick, Dutch wooden shoes, birdcage, barber shop pole, truck key, twizzler spoon, and golf club!

The population of this Illinois town is only 2,744 so the mayor created attractions to try and bring in more visitors, and it worked. Every weekend, the town attracts 1–2,000 people to come to view these amazing displays. So, I wonder what Matteo's invention has to do with this lady's interest in it. The plot thickens.

Then, Liam begins to share what he found on the cowboy guy with the white truck. He goes by Daniel Blackmann, a forty-four-year-old from Tuscola, Illinois, a town near Sarena's. He's trying to get his hands on this invention to make a profit. He has no record of endangering anyone before, but who's to say he's not the stabber? But how did they find out about the invention in the first place? Matteo seems pretty protective and secretive about it.

We agree that when Matteo is released tomorrow, Liam will come back to work out a plan with him and see if we can get more specifics from him. Meanwhile, Liam will try to keep tabs on Daniel to make sure he doesn't come snooping around or cause anyone harm. Maybe even snap a photo to show Matteo and see if he recognizes him as the one who attacked him in the night.

We pray together to put this whole incident into God's hands once again and ask for wisdom to guide us every step of the way. Liam asks how I am holding up under all this new stress, and I admit that I'm just living one day at a time and trying not to worry about tomorrow. It is easier said than done, but with God it is possible. I can rely on His strength in my weakness, but it seems like I'm feeling pretty weak at the moment.

I need to focus on going to work tomorrow, giving my best to my students, and trying not to be distracted. It's amazing how the human mind can compartmentalize events to block out the major stresses and go on with normal everyday life. I'm not really sure if it's a healthy way to cope with trauma. I can figure that out down the road when I have time to ponder everything after this is resolved.

"Thanks for stopping by, Liam, and thanks for wanting to help me out, even if it puts your job at risk. I appreciate you having my back." We walk toward the door. "You're the only person I can trust in the police department at the moment. I hope it isn't asking too much of you."

"No, I assure you," he says. "I'm a big boy and I can handle myself pretty well in the stealth department. Don't you worry about me. It's you I'm worried about protecting."

He bends down to give me a warm embrace, and I hang on tight, soaking in his ability to make me feel safe. He lets go of me first and promises to be in touch. I feel bereft but realize my clinginess is a sign that I need to hit the sack and get some rest.

CHAPTER FIVE

After an amazing full night's sleep of undisturbed bliss, I feel refreshed and ready to face my students with enthusiasm. I ask God for grace to face whatever challenges lie ahead, and I receive His grace by faith with a thankful heart.

I check in on the meowing kittens. Daisy, the mama cat gets an added treat because she has to nourish all these cuties. Bozer enjoys his dog food with beef bouillon stew drippings, and I throw a few fish crumbs to Marv the fish, who is always blowing me kisses. All fed and watered, I grab a chocolate shake and my book bag full of goodies. I head off in my Civic that will need some gas soon. Prices are starting to soar again at $163.9/L and I groan as I know inflation is still on the rise.

I allow the coastal drive to wash over my soul. I never tire of the ocean's beauty, its ever-changing hues of blue, gray, and green, or the waves either lapping or crashing depending on the wind. Today they are frothy with foam blowing onto my car, and I realize a storm is brewing. I hope I remembered to fold up my umbrella over the hot tub and button down anything that could fly away in this wind. I only teach for a few hours today, so I can return to check on things later.

My five students are eager to learn, and I love how everything else fades away to a background hum as I focus on each precious child. Of course, the school is abuzz with what they've seen on the news about the drowned woman and the stabbed stranger, and how they don't know what to make of it all. Ditto! Thankfully, the press has remained silent that the stranger was found on my front sidewalk, but the cat will be out of the bag before long. I gather my books, treats, stickers, and rhythm instruments as I head out the door, hoping to avoid too much chitchat so I can drive to the hospital to get Matteo home.

I feel like a spy out of a movie as I scan the parking lot for Daniel's white truck. I see nothing out of the ordinary, so I resume walking to my car and shift my focus. Now the background hum has turned into a loud symphony that I cannot ignore. It's time to face the music.

Mindy and Matteo are ready to go and eager to leave the hospital, but I need to get the doctor's final orders on how to treat the wound and any medication that he might need. Dr. Strahl explains the meds, and how to keep the wound clean. The doctor tells me to bring him back if I see any red welts, smell a foul odor, or if my patient develops a fever. He also warns that the police have been checking in every day and that I should expect visits. They've already been informed of my address and will want access to continue on the case. Great, so no flying under the radar. Maybe if things get dicey, I can move him to Brian's house or even Liam's without informing the police.

Mindy pushes Matteo in a wheelchair to the car, which is hard on his macho pride, so I try to smooth things over. "You've got this, Matteo. It's only necessary to baby the wound, but soon, you'll be a free man."

"I wish it were that simple, Marina. Right now I have to focus on recovery. And I have a long way to go before I feel free to accomplish my goals without being threatened by those who wish to stop me."

"We will help in any way we can," I assure him, "but first let's enjoy being free from the hospital and enjoy some country living, eh?"

"Sounds wonderful. I can't wait to cook, go for walks, and enjoy this beautiful paradise," Mindy says. She smiles wistfully and gazes out at the clear blue skies, fields, and ocean view.

"Just to let you know, I've prepared the guest room on the main floor for you, Matteo, so you don't have to navigate the stairs. Mindy will be right across the hall from you, and I will be upstairs in my usual room, as I have my own master suite. We'll have you all situated in no time," I declare.

The drive home is uneventful.

We're greeted by an excited Bozer. He is practically jumping into the car to give kisses to Matteo, who happily scratches him behind the ears and laughs at his exuberance.

"Bozer, so much for being a ferocious guard dog. You're supposed to give him a hard time," I exclaim. But maybe he remembers the wounded Matteo from Friday and is welcoming him home. Man, has it been only three days since that incident? It feels like I've aged a few years since then, as my twenty-three years feel a lot older right about now.

Mindy is so excited to explore the farm, have fresh veggies, and is looking forward to country living. I gladly let her take over my kitchen. I prefer to bake any day. I do have some canning still to do, mainly pickled beets, cucumbers, carrots, and beans. She is thrilled to learn the process and I will enjoy having the extra help. But we will save that work for another day, maybe Saturday.

Mindy has claimed the kittens, and they're purring up a storm for her. I warn her not to get too attached as I cannot keep them all through the winter. She is already picking her favorites and doesn't seem to even hear me.

Matteo seems happy to have a change of scenery and is looking out the big front bay window at the fields that have been harvested and the beautiful maples that are showing off their glorious reds. He is commenting on the huge cedar trees, and I am still in awe of the grandeur of the massive trees that stand like sentinels. I never tire of the green ferns that mostly survive through the winter and how lush the forest remains through the seasons. I hope I fare as well through this season of life that is taxing all my reserves.

It's a good thing the wind has died down and all is well on the home front with no shingles gone missing from the roof. My umbrella is still intact. The fallen leaves have blown about, but it's nothing a leaf blower and some raking can't fix. A workout would provide an outlet for my pent-up emotions. After Mindy's supper, I might be able to coax her to a hot tub soak and get to know their story and any clues I might pick up.

I enjoy raking the red maple leaves that are the size of my boot length and breathing in the crisp fall air. My guests might be up for a sunset ocean drive soon, but tonight they just want to relax over a delicious smelling croque monsieur with a garden salad tossed with a homemade Greek vinaigrette and some sautéed baby carrots.

"Ooh, I could get used to this kind of treatment," I declare.

Matteo is digging in with gusto. I know from experience that a full belly is a perfect time to ask him about his life, dreams, goals, and ambitions. So, I wait until dessert time. I nonchalantly ask over saskatoon pie with vanilla bean ice cream, "What is your line of work, and where is home base for you?"

"I am a research geneticist scientist and work at the University of Chicago," he replies naturally. "I hold lectures in my spare time and I'm on the cusp of a huge breakthrough. The lady that was murdered, Sarena, was a colleague of mine. She was instrumental in the developmental phase. We were here to meet with another scientist secretly. But obviously, we were compromised and can't trust our sources.

"Daniel is a new enemy that attended my lectures and, I assume, wants to build my prototype for his own personal gain. We're working on the patent with the scientist here. We need to proceed with caution and utmost secrecy."

"Do you think it was Daniel that stabbed you?" I ask.

"It's a good possibility, but he doesn't seem the type. Maybe he hired a hit man. He is very polished in the classroom, but the man you described chasing you sounds very boorish. So, that is another mystery to be solved, I'm afraid."

Mindy pipes in that perhaps once Matteo is recuperated, he can go hide on an island nearby and work in peace so as not to endanger anyone in Hillersby. "Do you know of a cabin somewhere?" she asks.

"Actually, I do have a friend who owns a cabin that overlooks the ocean on Sentry Island. He has a boat that can get you there when you feel ready."

"I do not want to be a burden on anyone," Matteo says. "So, I will pay him and be out of your hair so you can resume your life unencumbered by my mess. I just seem to create havoc and hurt those I get close to."

I assure him, "God must have a plan for him to have put us together on this new invention. Would it be possible to get more details so I can help or support you in any way?"

He laughs and placates me with, "Maybe later. But at the moment, it's too dangerous. It's best if fewer people know about it."

Drat! I thought he might say something to that effect, and I know that cajoling won't help my case. It is better to zip the lip and not beg. I just pray that he changes his mind soon.

So, I smile politely, nod, and say, "I can't wait for that day."

Matteo raises an eyebrow as if to question my agreeable nature. He thinks he's got me pegged already. Well, I think he's a little moody, but that could be due to his pain level.

He seems to genuinely care for others and wants to make a difference in this world to improve our way of life. And, he is ruggedly handsome with his soft, easy smile encompassing full lips that border his straight white teeth. I mustn't forget to mention his dimples that deepen when he smiles. He also has this full-throated laugh that emerges at times.

"Hey Matteo, your hands seem to be roughened by other work than just research and lab work. Where did you grow up and what else do you busy yourself with on the side?"

Mindy laughs at my direction of questions and coyly says, "Oh, he wasn't always a city boy. He grew up gold mining in Venezuela. His father wanted him to get a good education. His father was from a wealthy family, so he moved Matteo and his two sisters to the States when he was nineteen to attend university."

Mindy continues, "His mother was American and had dual citizenship, so they had a home in both countries and could benefit from both lifestyles. But Matty has always enjoyed working with his hands and figuring out solutions to everyday problems, hence his affinity for creating and inventing new ideas. He saw horrible working conditions in the gold mines and wanted to create easier ways to do mundane jobs. Thankfully, his father, Theodore, encouraged his abilities and gave him his own workshop to try out the ideas that always swirled in his brain."

"Fascinating, and what about your mother?" I ask innocently.

There is an awkward pause before Matteo gracefully recovers and explains that she died of ovarian cancer when he was seventeen, and that's when he decided to become a geneticist.

"Her suffering tore me up inside," He slowly explains. "I threw myself headlong into my studies, hoping to ease the pain. My two older sisters carved out lives for themselves in the States. My oldest sister is married with a toddler, and the other is happily single and studying to become an orthodontist."

I hastily empathize. "I'm so sorry. I hate cancer. It has claimed the lives of so many, caused untold suffering, and left us bereft. My dear father was another casualty just three short years ago. When will this ever stop?"

He agrees and expresses his sympathy for the passing of my father and for Mindy, who lost her sister (his mother) much too soon. His dear mother was only forty-five years old and left the family feeling helpless and robbed of a loved one much too soon.

Mindy begins to reminisce about all the good times they had and how those memories sustained her through the dark periods of grief and anger.

"I found journaling as a great way to walk through the pain and try to come to grips with the fact that God is still good. He can use all things for good even when you cannot see it at the time," Mindy says.

Matteo's eyes darken in intensity as he describes his outright refusal of a God that chose not to intervene and heal his mother. He eventually came around to the conclusion that God did not cause this disease. Therefore, God is not to be blamed.

Whew, their sharing touches a few raw nerves. I recall my own healing journey and how I still don't think I'm truly done grieving yet. I know I've experienced most of the five stages of grief, namely: denial, anger, bargaining, depression, and acceptance. But they seem to zing or visit me in no particular order and with no advance warning. I know I have the hope that I will see my father again and that he is having the time of his life in heaven. But trying to come to grips with the grisly way this disease caused him to suffer is really hard.

Matteo can't help but explain how the Greek word cancer comes from the word crab because of the finger-like projections as it spreads since it conjures up the shape of a crab. Cancer is a genetic disease caused by changes to the DNA when cells divide uncontrollably and spread into surrounding tissues. DNA damage can be caused by harmful substances in the environment, or it can be genetic.

"We probably don't need a science lesson tonight but thanks for sharing your input," Mindy teases. "Matty, we appreciate all that you do but it's time to hit the hay and let your body do some gene healing."

I laugh at her comment and get up to find them some towels and get them situated for the night. It gets dark early now, so I leave a few night lights on. I remember we were supposed to soak in the hot tub, but I guess that can wait for another day. Mindy still has to check Matteo's dressing, so I bid them a good night and hope it is non-eventful.

CHAPTER SIX

I awaken to darkness around 6:30 a.m., grateful that I had another undisturbed night of rest. I am ready to tackle the day. I take my coffee, do my daily devotion, take breakfast, and prepare a few lessons for my students whom I have the privilege of teaching today.

Oh wait, I do have house guests and they may need some pampering. I also want to offer my beater Chevy truck to Mindy in case she'd like to run a few errands. I have no idea if they're going to sleep in or when I should prepare breakfast, so I get myself ready first. The shower feels heavenly until I get a blast of cold water signifying that my guests are up. I quickly throw on some jeggings and a long red cozy plaid, throw my hair in a messy bun and apply a little foundation to cover the black bags under my eyes. Guess I need more beauty sleep.

Mindy is busily humming her way around some fried eggs, bacon, and hash browns when I come downstairs. Wow, she gets ready quickly in the morning. She also sounds like a morning person. "How was your sleep?" I cheerily ask. "I know it can be elusive when you're in a strange house for the first night."

"Oh, super great. I slept like a log and only got up once to check on Matty, but he was busy snoring. I didn't have the heart to wake him to check on his bandages. I think it's a good sign that he's on the mend if he can get a full night's sleep in."

"Well, you can borrow my green truck out there if you need to go anywhere. The keys are hanging in the laundry room and I don't use it very often, so it's all yours."

"Bless your heart, I think I will stay put today as your fridge is well-stocked. I do want to pay for your next grocery run and I would love to do the shopping."

"Sure thing. Do you need help with breakfast, although it looks like you have it all under control?"

"Ha, I love to cook, so this is me playing house. Thank you for giving me the freedom. I feel right at home. It'll be ready in five minutes. Oh, and I already fed the pets as they were begging. I couldn't resist. Even the fish got some love."

"Amazing. I am really going to enjoy having you stick around and I'm looking forward to getting to know you better too. Can we have a girl date tonight in the hot tub after supper? We can enjoy the stars and maybe some northern lights. I heard it's supposed to be clear skies tonight and quite the show!"

"Yes, that sounds wonderful. Can you keep your eyes on the bacon? I need to check on Matty and see if he's ready to partake."

I happily flip the sizzling bacon and begin to plan my day with what I might need for my classes. I'm surprised to see my automatic light go on by the garage outside. I check to see if it was tripped by a deer, but I don't see anything with four legs. I see one with two legs, and he's looking right at me with a dazed expression like a deer caught in headlights.

I shout and grab my bat by the door, calling for Bozer while I fly out the door, hoping to chase this interloper off my land. Bozer runs ahead of me, barking ferociously, and by the time I make it to the garage, there is no sign of the intruder. How did he disappear like that?

I can still hear Bozer in hot pursuit, but then he stops barking and comes back running to me unharmed but with no prize. We turn back to the house to find an anxious Mindy and a very alarmed Matteo, whose eyes are spitting fire at me.

"Don't ever charge out there again without backup. You could've been hurt! We don't know who we're dealing with yet or if he's dangerous." He calms down a little. "Please wait until I recover or I've come up with a plan to entice him out of hiding," he pleads.

I amusedly chuckle. I'm not used to being babied or handled with kid gloves, but it's kind of nice for a change. It's also a little irritating. I don't like being told what I can or can't do on my own turf. I guess we all have some adjusting to do when sharing our space with others.

Mindy rushes in to give me a hug and commend me for my bravery. "However, I think it was a tad irresponsible not to wait for backup," she says.

Hmm, she sounds like my mother, and I miss my mom, so I guess I'll let it slide for today. I assure them I can take care of myself, but I will try to use wisdom next time and assess the danger before I act impulsively. That seems to pacify them for the moment, so I redirect their attention to breakfast, which now smells like overdone eggs. However, the crispy bacon is just the way I like it.

Matteo discusses with Mindy his plans for the day, which involves more research. I suggest we invite Liam over to plan our next move to get on the same page. "Maybe he could come over for supper and we can see if he's had any more luck with sleuthing out the truth. I could pick up a roasted chicken, and we could add some garden veggies, a chef's salad, and homemade biscuits. What do you guys think?"

"Sure, sounds like a good plan to me," Mindy says, approvingly. Matteo nods his head and proceeds to his room to get right to work.

I hurriedly gather my bag and head to school, hoping to run into Linda, who teaches the second graders. She already went through a harried night at my place and can help bring some perspective to ground me today. I know she has a break at 10:30 a.m. I should be able to catch her for ten minutes before I teach piano to my eager students.

As I head to the break room, I pray for privacy and help to focus. The scare this morning has me on edge. Lindy is just warming up a cinnamon bun when I walk in. She gives me a huge hug that reaches my toes and settles me down so I can explain everything. She is concerned about another trespasser and wants me to move into town with her. I thank her for the offer but assure her that I don't feel too badly shaken up yet and that I hope to find answers as we involve Liam's help. She's relieved. She asks if I will bring Matteo to church so the soul sisters can meet him. They want to see if he is good boyfriend material for me, but that is the furthest thing from my mind right now. It is too complicated to even go down that path of rose petals and potential heartache. Linda chimes in that love is always on time and that I shouldn't close that door. She knows this firsthand since she is dating Pastor Ted's son, Carl, who is dream boyfriend material. I sigh and say that not everyone gets to be courted like she is! We agree to keep in touch and to remind ourselves that this too shall pass eventually. Right now, it feels like a long night of the soul. I will need to walk by the ocean to rejuvenate and clear my head after I teach.

The students are a little on edge today and having a hard time concentrating, so I add music games and singing to change the tone and brighten their day. Prizes and candy are good motivators too. They must be sensing the uncertainty and worry of their parents because our once calm town is feeling a little unsettled by the unsolved cases. This reminds me to text Liam and invite him over for supper and to stop by the store for some hot chicken. But I have a window of time to drive to the closest beach that is known for its oyster shells. Maybe I can snag a few for supper if it's not red tide. If you eat shellfish during red tide and get a tingling sensation, seek medical help as you may be suffering from PSP (paralytic shellfish poisoning), which can be life-threatening. However, the algae bloom usually occurs in the spring and summer months, so we should be safe, I hope.

The ocean is a blue-gray color today. The tide brought in a lot of seaweed from the storm, so the air is rife with briny smells. I go for a brisk walk along the shore. Looking for neat shells is a perfect diversion to refuel my batteries. That is my perfect idea of a date. I pride myself that I will be a low-maintenance, inexpensive girlfriend when the time is right. Gloria, my mom, would also add that I am quite a prize, but she might be a tad biased.

I am quite happy with my find of ten massive oyster shells. Two would fill me up. My guests will be quite thrilled to try the delicacies of the sea. Maybe I don't need chicken at all tonight. I am a hunter-gatherer at heart and have even tried eating raw seaweed. It's a little gritty but nice and salty.

I feel God's peace begin to permeate my soul just by taking time to focus on Him and His beautiful creation that I am surrounded by. I have chosen to never take them for granted. I begin to sing Romans 15:13, which has a great promise: "Now may God, the fountain of hope, fill you to overflowing with uncontainable joy and perfect peace as you trust in him. And may the power of the Holy Spirit continually surround your life with his super-abundance until you radiate with hope!" Yes, I receive His hope, joy, peace, and power to sustain me through this season.

Feeling refreshed, I zip back home to show off my find and get started on supper, only to find Mindy happily puttering away. All that's left to do is cook the oysters and set the table.

"Thanks for helping me get supper ready for our guest tonight," I gratefully say.

"Well, our day consisted mostly of resting and recuperating, so we're in fine form to feast on your fresh seafood. We're also looking forward to meeting Liam," replies Mindy.

I hear a knock at the door and run to open it to find not Liam but Brian standing there. Surprised, I invite him in to join us and set another spot at the table as he warmly greets Mindy and Matteo. They bring him up to speed on Matteo's health progress, and Brian encourages them to stop by and visit his farm sometime.

The doorbell rings, allowing Liam to join in on the fray, and we all sit down to partake. I ask Liam to say grace and we all dig in with gusto. The oysters are deliciously served with garlic butter. I even spot the beginnings of a pearl in mine. So neat. The banter is light while we enjoy the juicy corn on the cob, warm biscuits that melt in your mouth, and chef's salad, just enough for all of us to feel satisfied. To complete our meal, Brian pulls out lemon squares that he bought at the bakery to satisfy our palates.

Time to get down to business and see what Liam has found out this week.

"I was able to track Daniel, the white truck driver, and managed to snap his photo to enable Matteo to confirm his identity." He shows the photo to Matteo. "Is this the same polished guy from the classroom or not?"

"No!" sputters Matteo as his eyes grow wide at the big burly man in the photo.

"How can this be?" I wonder aloud. "They have the same name, but it's not the same guy. Why is he using Daniel's identity as an alias, and where is the real Daniel? Who is this guy?"

"His frame matches the guy who stabbed me, but it was dark. I can't be certain it was this pretender," Matteo says.

"The plot thickens once again. Instead of providing answers, we have created more questions. What are the police doing and how is their investigation coming along?" I muse.

Brian seems put off after seeing the picture, and the rest of us are puzzled. We might have to sleep on this one and hope for inspiration or clarity come morning.

Liam promises to discreetly ask at the precinct and takes his leave with Brian closely on his heels. That leaves us girls to clean up as Matteo is exhausted and is forced to retire early. Mindy offers to change his dressing, noting with satisfaction that the wound is still clear of any infection. We wash the dishes in record time as the hot tub is calling our names and we just want to soak our cares away.

There is nothing like stepping into 101 degrees Fahrenheit of hot blissfulness to soothe the frayed nerves and cause a sigh of thankfulness for the finer things in life. We hash out all the possibilities and then change topics altogether to enjoy the evening of shining stars and a hint of green northern lights dancing across the skies in the distance. Bozer is off chasing a rabbit or raccoon, and hopefully, Matteo is snoring already. We enjoy our girl talk and tell stories late into the night until it feels like our skin is getting wrinkly.

Then, I can't help but tell her about the time when I was a teenager. "I was cross country skiing in the field, enjoying the blue skies when, all of a sudden, I panicked because I spotted a big black bear in the distance. I hurriedly took off my skis. Since I was a beginner skier, I reasoned I could better outrun the bear than out ski him." Mindy laughs quietly. "I nearly peed my pants during the process because I was so scared."

Mindy interrupts with a guffaw, but I signal with my finger to bear with me until I finish my story.

"I had to creep closer to get back to the house. I scampered behind a tree and peered around the trunk to see if it had sniffed out my location yet. Nope, being upwind was to my advantage, which gave me a small sense of comfort. So, I began to plan my best route of escape when, lo and behold, the wind picked up and the bear began to flutter! How can this be? I squinted to make sure my eyes were not playing tricks on me. I could not believe what they seemed to be telling me. It was a big black garbage bag fluttering in the breeze, caught on a barbwire fence! I was so disgusted with the trickery that I threw my skis in the snow and screamed in frustration at how I had been duped by a dumb garbage bag. I was furious at my own stupidity and how I'd succumbed to my own irrational fears instead of being relieved that there was no danger lurking about after all."

Mindy is splitting her guts laughing and can't believe how gullible I was to fall for that, but I assure her it looked very real! Just then, an owl hoots. We both jump and scream, then laugh. It feels so good to be lighthearted and not have any worries for a few hours at least.

CHAPTER SEVEN

Wednesday dawns with a gorgeous sunrise that I take in with my coffee while reading Hebrews 2:14-15. It describes how Jesus became human to fully identify with us and experienced death to set us free from the fear of death. Death has no power or dominion over me, and I have no fear of it as He conquered it at the cross to deliver me from Satan's hold. I have amazing freedom and the ability to grab hold of this promise for this current situation that I'm facing right now. I have nothing to fear because I trust in Him completely. I have His resurrection life flowing through me to vanquish every foe. I can change the atmosphere by speaking His life-giving words, such as Romans 8:37-38: "Yet even in the midst of all these things, we triumph over them all, for God has made us to be more than conquerors, and his demonstrated love is our glorious victory over everything! So now I live with the confidence that there is nothing in the universe with the power to separate us from God's love. I'm convinced that his love will triumph over death, life's troubles, fallen angels, or dark rulers in the heavens. There is nothing in our present or future circumstances that can weaken his love." Amen!

I sense someone watching me and notice Matteo standing in the dark hallway. He slowly enters when he notices that I've seen him.

"Good morning!" I greet him excitedly. "You're walking on your own. You must be feeling better!"

"Yes, thank you. I can tell I have to be careful though. No sit-ups yet, but my strength is returning. Hey, I noticed the peace on your face when you were reading. Care to share which part caught your attention?"

I share my thoughts and he is moved but seems guarded somehow. I am guessing he was hurt by religion or religious people and is still on the path of needing to forgive, release, and discover truths for himself. He is still hesitant to share his journey, but I can wait and will pray for angels to be sent to serve and care for him to be open to receiving salvation (Hebrews 1:14). I think he knows he needs to be saved from his sins; that is, to confess out loud that Jesus is Lord and believe in his heart that God raised Jesus from the dead. But something is holding him back from receiving this gift of righteousness (Romans 10:9).

"Thanks for sharing. I appreciate it, but I can't seem to come to terms with a God who is loving and yet allows bad things to happen to good people and vice versa. I get the fact that we have free will. I mean, look at Satan. He was the highest angel, and yet pride entered him. He fell, and that's how evil came to be. But God could've superseded him, yet He already knew this would happen and had plan B ready: to send Jesus as a baby to rescue us from the power of Satan. We can now live free from sin but look at how corrupted people have become in starting wars, human trafficking, murder, and downright evil. Free will is horrifying. It can be beautiful when we choose to love, forgive, and turn the other cheek, but where is justice? It must break God's heart to see us reject His son over and over and harden our hearts to the truth."

Whoa, his depth and understanding are quite amazing. He looks like he just surprised himself with his own answer just by expressing his thoughts out loud.

"That is quite insightful, Matteo. I think you're closer to the truth than you thought. I think the Holy Spirit is showing you even now that your pathway to freedom involves saying yes to Him and forgiving yourself and others who have hurt you along the way."

"Yes, I suppose it is something I will have to work out with Him over time. And, the quiet and reprieve I feel here is something I haven't experienced in a long time. My life was always so busy, filled with this invention and trying to get it right, that I never stopped to think through my own bitterness and anger at God for taking my mom too soon and not healing her. I guess your story of similar grief touched my heart and made me revisit my own reactions. I am so consumed by this that I need to take a step back and re-evaluate."

"I appreciate your honesty and willingness to go there. It takes courage, openness, and vulnerability. I'm always on a quest for the truth myself, hoping to eradicate unbelief from my heart, keep a cleansed conscience, and not get easily offended."

"Easier said than done, I'd say, but a noble quest and one we shall have to resume as I have some more digging to do."

I concur. I'm embarrassed when my stomach lets out a huge growl as we can both smell Mindy's breakfast swirling down the hall. We laugh and decide to partake together when the doorbell rings. It's strange to have visitors this early in the morning, which can mean only one thing. Yes, I guessed it. The police have come to investigate the case and question us about more evidence that they found. I might be late for work, but maybe I can be excused rather quickly once I say my spiel.

Liam is not among them, which makes me think we should be discreet and not volunteer more information than what they ask. I can see Matteo is on the same wavelength by the raised eyebrow look that he sends my way. I nod imperceptibly as we invite them to eat with us. Food is an amazing tool to soften anyone's heart, or so I've heard. Let's put this saying to the test.

They accept our invitation with enthusiasm, so I rise to brew a fresh pot of strong coffee and help Mindy scramble more eggs. The biscuits and sausage will suffice as the three guys have probably already had their first breakfast at home. We enjoy a few minutes of banter before we get down to business.

They zero in on Sarena and her relationship with Matteo. He assures them that he knew her from his lectures only and that they were just colleagues. They seem to accept the fact that they were friends, as they are suspecting someone else as the murderer.

"Do you recognize or know anyone going by the name of Daniel Blackmann?"

Matteo describes the Daniel he knows as an African American man who attended his lectures. He was just an acquaintance and didn't really know much about him. They ask for specifics on his build, complexion, and height and then proceed to show a picture of the white truck driver that doesn't match the description at all. Something fishy is going on here just as we suspected. They seem clueless as to the reason why we have a masquerade going on with a fake identity. More digging is required on both ends, but they reassure us that they will handle this themselves.

The questioning turns to whether Matteo can remember anything new from the night of his attack and whether he can identify the physique matching the picture of the fake Daniel.

"I cannot affirm it 100 percent as it was dark and the man had a hood on, but the build seems similar."

To conclude, they would like to be apprised of Matteo's whereabouts at all times so they can question him further as new evidence comes into play. We thank them for their time and I see them to the door. I breathe a sigh of relief as they drive away with full bellies but not much else to go on.

The mood is somber as I return to clean up the dishes. Mindy is muttering under her breath, and Matteo excuses himself to the privacy of his bedroom. I give her a hug and offer to drive them to the beach for a sunset on the water and maybe some takeout to enjoy after my workday is done. She agrees and distracts herself by playing with the kittens, and I remind her not to get too attached as I may only keep one and give the rest away. Maybe I should bring them to school and let the students pick some out for themselves, after they get permission from their parents, of course. She is snuggling a gray cat with blue eyes that I secretly favor as well. I named her Beautiful, but of course, I love the ginger ones too. We will both be sad when we have to say goodbye, but such is life on the farm.

My students are back to their bouncy selves and ready to engage in their lessons, which makes my job a delight. I love how I can get in the zone with them and forget about the stresses back home. It is so rewarding to see children achieve their goals, become confident, compose themselves, and express their emotions. I feel such a bond as I've taught some of them since they were five years old, and after six years of sharing music together, I think of them as "my kids." I am so glad my mom pushed me when I wanted to quit and encouraged me when the going got tough. I've been teaching since I was sixteen years old and really love what I do. I think it's important in life to find your passion and pursue it, and to help others figure out what makes them come alive.

Susan is my eleven-year-old student who has a natural talent. She puts in the practice time and enjoys making music, whereas Sally slogs through her lessons. Sally is quite good when she plays by ear but she detests reading notes. Therefore, I still teach both ways but encourage her to explore songs she wants to learn while still practicing her lesson book.

I am prepping my forty-five students for a Christmas recital and would like to start them early so they can learn a few songs and then pick their favorites to perform. My career is teaching music to young children. I can teach six students at a time with six keyboards, so lessons can get pretty intense sometimes. I teach rhythm instruments, solfege, listening activities as well as chording and composing. I also help lead the choir, and teach singing, ukulele, and sometimes, the accordion. I feel like the pied piper as I play in the halls and during recess as the children follow behind me dancing to the beat. Such fun, entertaining and rewarding work, or dare I say play!

I begin to think about Matteo's work and how fulfilling it must be to create something new. I can't wait until he trusts me enough to want to share his whole creative journey with me. I realize his hesitation is because he wants to protect me. The fewer people that know, the better. And no one can steal his ideas, but he must realize who he's dealing with here. Innocent Moi! Time will tell if he chooses to let his guard down and let me in. I know Mindy is privy to the inside scoop. I wonder if he has trusted other family members with it or not. I guess I would be tight-lipped too if I were in his shoes, on the cusp of revealing the invention to the world. I would not want anyone to steal my thunder or get the credit.

Wait, I see my truck in the parking lot. Ah, they must've driven in to save me a trip and are ready to go for our sunset picnic by the ocean. I bet Mindy already picked up the food she was craving. I am guessing it is pad Thai, which I also enjoy. My taste buds are watering just thinking about it. I remember I skipped lunch, so I am feeling famished.

I wave at them to follow me, but they are motioning me over with the window rolled down. I hastily jog to my truck and notice a warning of fear in their eyes. As I get closer, I see fake Daniel sitting behind them with a gun aimed at Matteo's neck. He motions me to sit beside him in the backseat. What is going on here?

He orders Mindy to drive to the ocean and is looking a little crazed. I debate whether to make a scene or scream, but I'm afraid he will pull the trigger and I don't want to endanger Matt's life. I can't believe I came up with his nickname at a time like this, but all my senses are in overdrive. I'm praying like crazy for wisdom on how to get out of this alive and unscathed. God help!

I can tell Matt is about to do something silly to try and protect us, so I begin to pray out loud. This confuses Daniel and he orders me to stop. So, I begin to sing while Mindy is driving alarmingly fast since she is a ball of nerves and fuming mad. Daniel commands me to be silent or he will knock the living daylights out of me, which I believe he might deliver any second.

I decide to be brave and ask him, "What is your real name, and why are you assuming someone else's identity?"

You can tell he's been hired for his brawn and not his brains as he gets all flustered and sputters, "I am who I say I am and why would you th…think otherwise?"

He barks at Mindy to turn left, then right down a hidden overgrown path that leads to a sheltered cove. The car comes to a stop and he orders us to get out first.

This is our chance to distract him, get a message out to Liam on my phone, scream, run, or all the above. What to do first?

Mindy has the foresight to take the keys with her. She locks it, and purposefully sets the truck alarm off, giving Matt a chance to elbow the gun out of Daniel's hand. Matt headbutts him and jumps out of the truck before Daniel recovers. What a fiasco!

He checks to make sure the ladies are safe and grabs some rope to tie up the unconscious dude before he wakes up and causes more trouble.

So much for enjoying a relaxing picnic and watching the sunset. It is a spectacular work of art at the moment if I might add. I text Liam while Mindy is wildly looking around for an escape route, hoping help is on the way.

Daniel groans as he begins to stir and starts to thrash around to get free. He stops as he realizes it's hopeless. His eyes are black with fury as he begins to spew malicious threats about what he is going to do to us. Matt threatens to knock him out cold again but instead, grabs him, gags him, and throws him into the back of the truck.

Silence at last.

Liam should be here any moment. I'm looking forward to some answers about what this fake Daniel is after. I want to know if he is the only one that knows about this or if there are others. We stop to listen as we hear a vehicle coming down the trail, but it doesn't sound like a diesel engine, and I wonder how anyone else would know we're here. Coming out from among the trees is a ghost truck with two of the same three policemen we fed breakfast to that very morning! Great, we'll be having a party soon once Liam shows up, as he probably called Brian for backup too.

We wave to acknowledge them, but they seem to be taking in the scene looking for someone, so I point to the back of the truck that is shaking from side to side with our roller who is trying to free himself. They quickly jump out, grab Daniel, and tell us they will be in touch, and that they got it from here. What? No questioning, no concern, no details, nada! Strange indeed.

Matteo is taking this all in. "I wish we would've had time to question Daniel ourselves, but I'm pretty sure he wouldn't have been forthcoming." He frowns. "He would've lied through his teeth anyhow, but now I feel gypped. Sorry, Marina, that we were forced to involve you in this charade, in addition to your plans for a nice evening being thwarted. We'll make it up to you later, including getting some takeout for tonight when we pick up your car. I'm sure you're famished by now."

I nod and start babbling about how I can't believe Daniel would force them to drive my truck. I stop talking and begin to wonder what would have happened if he had the chance to go through with whatever he had planned. Would we be dead or alive? I then realize I am beginning to shake as the adrenaline begins to wear off. Mindy quickly supports me and motions for Matt to support my other side as they help me to the truck so I can sit and drink some water.

Mindy begins to murmur soothing words as she runs her fingers through my hair like my mother would do if she were here. Matt grabs the keys to drive, backs up, and tells me to drink in the view of the sunset or just close my eyes and lay my head on his shoulder. I opt for a bit of both. I'm thankful that I don't have to be brave at all times. I am surprised that I don't mind feeling weak in front of them. It's kind of nice to be myself and not feel like I need to pretend to be perfect. I can just be. I can show them the real me and still be accepted and loved. Well, maybe "loved" is a strong word, but "liked" is pretty good too.

As we're rounding a bend in the road, I see Liam's truck coming towards us alarmingly fast, with Brian in the co-driver seat hanging onto the handle above his head, looking grim. We stop, roll down the window, and hurriedly explain that we're all OK, but that the two cops have Daniel in custody. The boys are shocked at how the cops knew to come to this location, as Liam hadn't tipped them off. My text came while they were having coffee, so they came straight away.

I thank them, explain our plans, and welcome them to join us. Brian suggests we come to his house for some stew that he's been marinating in his slow cooker, so we don't have to go buy food and we can reconvene at the farm. We agree and decide to leave my car in town for the night so we can take a shortcut to Brian's and get some sustenance to plan our next move.

CHAPTER EIGHT

Matteo wants some time at the cabin to get away from any pursuers and have some intense concentration time to finish his prototype. I understand his frustration, so I call in a huge favor from my friend Rocky, who is probably halfway across the world on some adventure trip or another.

Rocky responds immediately, informing us where the keys are for his boat and cabin. He tells us to bring supplies as it is bare bones at the moment. He is so easy-going and laid back, which I am very thankful for at this time.

"What are you up to these days?" I ask.

He responds, "Rock climbing in New Zealand, enjoying the rugged mountains, and meeting new people."

I thank him profusely while he jokingly suggests I take him out for dinner when he gets back so he can dazzle me with all his adventures. Done. Not a problem. Matteo is wondering about the strings attached to this offer, and I assure him that Rocky is a good guy and very generous.

So, I take Friday off work to help Matt get set up on Sentry Island. Mindy offers to bring me to work today and buy him some supplies, which will give us one day to get organized. Of course, we don't even discuss this with the boys as Matt wants total secrecy. Just us girls know about it, and we will keep it that way for as long as we can.

Liam and Brian are busy with a few ideas of their own to get to the truth about fake Daniel. They promise to report back to us pronto. They will not be impressed when they find out what we have been up to, but all in the name of progress, I say. I can butter them up with a nice juicy steak and some mushroom caps stuffed with crab and cream cheese. That ought to suffice.

I figure this is a good time to hide Matt while Daniel is in custody, so we can sneak away, so to speak. I am worried Matt may get lonely out there. There is not much habitation on the island except for birds, sea lions, and a few other cabins on the north shore. The allotted structures allowed on the island are ten dwellings because of its small size. Rocky happened to inherit this land from his grandfather, and I am sure it will be kept in his generational line for as long as possible.

Matt assures me he loves solitude. Moreover, he needs it to complete his work, and he promises to share it with me after it's all said and done. I don't believe there is much reception there, so I will have to check in on him every few days to communicate. Mindy and I will have to be patient. She doesn't seem to be chomping at the bit to go back home. I figure the people she left in charge of her business and house must be very dependable and will receive good compensation for their efforts. She had shared that most of her business could be done online from anywhere, as she likes to be a free bird.

The day flies by with eager students plunking out their Christmas tunes, hoping to be the star of the show at the upcoming recital. I run into Linda, who is looking harried after spending all morning trying to pacify six-year-olds who are high-strung and need to run outside to get their jitters out. I laud her patience in dealing with twenty-eight students at once, while my max is only six. However, she gushes over my talent to be able to teach younger ones to create such pretty music. The good Lord has blessed us with gifts for His designed purpose, and it's great to recognize the passion He's placed inside us. That's what I love about teaching. I get to find the hidden talents in each student and bring them out.

Linda queries about Matteo's progress, and I simply mention that he is recovering well. We agreed that even my soul sisters could not know his whereabouts, which might prove tricky unless I can steer the meetings away from my place for now. I figure I can hedge for a few weeks, but then she innocently remarks, "I hope Matt can make it to church this Sunday so we can all lay eyes on him and be convinced that he is not a figment of your imagination."

I laugh and say, "I am working on him but he wants to keep a low profile as we don't know who we're dealing with yet regarding his attacker and the unsolved murder case of Sarena. Poor soul."

She accedes to that point and offers any help whatsoever. This reminds me to ask if we can meet at her place for our next soul sister meetup.

"Of course, I'll organize and set it up with the girls. No problem at all."

"I have to run and check on my guests. I look forward to our next rendezvous."

I rush home as I know that Mindy would've bought the supplies Matt needs. I can bring him to the island while there's still daylight. Mindy wants to come for the boat ride to help set him up but she wants to leave him space to create, so she will come back with me. I am happy she'll keep me company. I know I will feel safer if I'm not alone at home. Also, Matt will feel better knowing I have Mindy by my side if he can't be there to offer added protection. I guess it's only been six days since this all began last Friday. Today is only Thursday, but it feels like a month of intense activity has occurred.

I am greeted by Bozer, welcoming me with his usual dog talk, as if I've been gone for a week, which I find very amusing. I reciprocate by showering him with affection. As I enter my house, I see that totes are packed and ready to be loaded, efficiently marked with labels: Food, bedding, survival supplies, books, computer, and clothes. I am amazed at how much work they got accomplished. Matt looks like a kid ready to go on an adventure, and Mindy is dressed for the boat ride with a slicker in case it rains. I waste no time in changing my attire to suit the elements. It was so thoughtful of her to pack me supper so I could eat on the go.

I ask, "Did Liam call to give you any new leads on Daniel yet?"

They both respond with a negative head shake, and I sigh. I suspect more is going on than meets the eye. It will be hard to decipher the truth if the police are trying to hide something. Matt seems to know that undercurrents and greed are happening at high levels, as he's seen this before in his hometown with the gold mining operation. I decide that worrying will not solve any problems. I deliberately choose to cast my cares on God, trusting that He's got this.

I think I might miss Matt just a little. I have gotten used to having him around. I enjoy our talks, but I must let him go for the greater good, I suppose. He notices me watching him and a smile slowly spreads across his full lips, as if he can read my thoughts. The nerve! My cheeks get flushed, so I hastily look away to distract myself.

"Why are you guys standing about not packing the truck?" Mindy asks as she breezes past.

Right. It's nice to have a drill sergeant around to get us moving. I notice her sending a wink to Matt. She seems to have noticed the subtle attraction between us. I mean, I've only known him for barely a week, so it can't be much more than that. I've known Liam and Brian for years and I consider them good friends. They might vie for my attention, but it's all pretty harmless. Don't get me wrong, I do enjoy being single but I'm open to God opening the romance door when the time is right. My view is that I'm still young and have lots of time before I have to make up my mind about love.

I better get packing. My daydreaming has cost me valuable daylight. Off to the races. Hopefully, the ocean will be calm. Drat! I forgot to check the tides to make sure I can get the boat out of the marina. I flip open my phone to my saved bookmarked tidal chart page. I'm relieved to see that the low tide is mostly on its way back up, so I can relax.

Mindy offers to drive as she's gotten used to my old truck. I comply so I can eat my yummy supper that smells like pork souvlaki drizzled with tzatziki sauce, my favorite! Mindy and Matteo are humored by my groanings of satisfaction as I devour the scrumptious wrap. I thank her for spoiling me.

"Did you happen to know it was my favorite, Mindy?" I ask as I take another bite.

"Nope, but it's one of ours too and a good standby staple in our diet, so I figured you might enjoy it," Mindy responds, looking pleased as punch that I like her cooking.

Matt offers, "I wanted to thank you both for bending over backward to make this happen, for keeping it under wraps, and for providing all the supplies. I will repay you in kind soon. I am thrilled to be so close to completion and to have a space to perfect it. It means the world to me. I will miss you both for your excellent companionship, but focus is necessary for this final phase."

His eyes are scanning the roads and mirrors to make sure we're not being followed throughout the car ride. We are relieved to get to the marina undetected. I notice the coast guard boat is pulling in and the hustle and bustle is normal for a Thursday afternoon.

I motion for Matt to get the wheelbarrow nearby so we can load the totes and wheel them down the ramp to our awaiting vessel. Of course, I grab it from him so he doesn't reopen his wound. I'm pretty certain that the cabin will have a first aid kit if he needs extra bandages. I lead the way past the vast array of different types of boats that I love to peruse: working boats, prawning boats, sailboats, and yachts. Ours is a blue fishing boat that is easy to start and maneuver.

I always thought walking along the dock at night, with all the lights and the moon shining on the sea while watching the sunset would be so romantic. I would watch others who had the same idea and think this is just like in the movies. Here I go again, getting all side-tracked. I should concentrate or I will end up catapulting into the ocean with my totes floating around me if I'm not careful.

As we approach the boat, I see we will have to remove the canvas covering the deck and search to see if the key is in its hiding spot. Yes, everything seems to be well maintained and the key is right where it should be. The tank is full of gas, so all we have to do is load up our totes and push off.

What a glorious feeling to be on the water. It's so calming and it's like soothing oil to my soul. I feel free of any problems. I take in a deep breath of the tangy, salty air, and marvel at how the ocean looks as calm as glass. Serene!

I can see the effect it is having on my co-passengers as they drink in the beauty of the islands, the snow-covered mountains in the distance, and the seagulls singing their songs. Ah, peace is not highly overrated, it is heavenly indeed. Our wake from the boat is creating nice waves and a pod of dolphins begin to jump and dazzle us with their dance. I never tire of seeing all the beauty of creation that surrounds us.

It takes about forty-five minutes to get to Sentry Island by boat, so we settle in for the trip bundled against the wind. We're grateful for the Benini top on this boat, which shields us from most of the wind. I love handling the boat, but I allow Matt the chance to drive as he looks eager to do so. Mindy might want a turn on the way back as well. It's hard to carry a conversation as a person would have to shout to be heard above the roar of the motor, so we're content to look around for any signs of whales, seals, or more dolphins. Matt is doing zigzags on the water, but the little kid inside of him calms down to a straight course once more as he follows the GPS route mapped out for him.

In no time at all, it seems, we're approaching the dock. It's built for just this cabin, so there's no problem maneuvering the boat to tie it up securely and begin unloading. We have about thirty steps to climb up the bank that leads to the path through the trees to the cabin that is "chic rustic" in style. It is a timber frame with a loft, a cozy woodstove, and bay windows overlooking the ocean with a view that is to die for.

I remember where Rocky stashes the key. I open the door and proceed to give my guests the grand tour. Matt is impressed and is looking forward to unpacking and setting up. I think Mindy seems to want to stay too, but I am keeping an eye on the horizon as I know how quickly a storm can blow in.

I take the time to bring in some firewood, start a fire and make sure everything is in working order. Matt declares that this is the perfect place for him to be inspired and have the space to create. I mention that the storage shed is full of tools and that he is free to use whatever he finds. I hear an owl hoot and notice that time is slipping away on us as it gets dark earlier now.

I plug in the radio, locate a station, and tune in. We immediately hear a weather warning for a storm that is coming our way. Hmm, do we take a chance or should we hunker down for the night and make do? My animals are fine for one night. We fed them supper before we left, and we could leave at sunrise. We discuss our options, and Matt agrees that he doesn't want us to risk it.

"I suppose I can share my space for one night," he gregariously comments, sending a wink our way.

I punch him on the shoulder, and he fakes his injury by groaning in pain as if I really hurt him. Ha! Two can play this game. We scrounge up extra bedding and make our beds in the loft so Matt can have the comfortable bottom bedroom and not have to scale up the steep ladder. Mindy proceeds to make us a bedtime snack of a pickle wrapped with ham and a layer of cream cheese snugged with a toothpick, et voilà, a wonderful appetizer.

It's so nice to be wrapped in a blanket by the crackling fire, with hot cocoa, a book from Rocky's library, and our tasty hors d'oeuvres. I wasn't expecting to stay overnight, but this has turned out to be quite therapeutic and a break from all the happenings. I let out a long sigh, sounding like a cat purring out her contentment.

They look at me questioningly.

"What?" I counter. "I am just enjoying this time and making the most of our delayed situation."

They laugh but both agree with my musings. Life is like a roller coaster ride. I thrill at the variety and adventure, and I allow the down times to shape perseverance, character, and hope in me (Romans 5:4).

We start playing Rummy-O, as I love number games, and soon competition starts to kick in full force on all sides. Oh dear, we are all stubborn with strong personalities, but then again, those might be the very character traits that we need to survive all this. Of course, it's hard to beat Matt's mind at a numbers game, but we had fun trying.

I notice that we're all yawning so I call it a night and go hunker down in our cozy loft. Matt pulls one of my curls as he struts by with his winning title and wishes us a good night.

So much for not rubbing it in. I can't let him get the last word in, so

I challenge him, "I will win one of these times soon."

"I look forward to it and then we must celebrate," is his mocking reply.

Cocky and confident too!

"Good night."

CHAPTER NINE

I toss and turn throughout the night. I can hear the storm raging. I get up twice to keep the fire going in the woodstove, so we don't freeze. I am not a night owl and much prefer the mornings.

I could just picture my dad playing the violin in the air with his big fingers, mocking my grumpiness. I can't help but smile to myself as a reminder to not complain. Yes, others have it much worse, and I am blessed and have so much to be thankful for. I do miss my papa and I picture him looking down on me from heaven, hopefully praying for his loved ones, in between all his heavenly adventures, of course.

My parents miscarried three babies, so it comforts me to think that he is having a grand time with his three children already up there. What a reunion that must have been! I can't wait to meet my three brothers when it's my turn to graduate.

I must've fallen back asleep. I awaken to the smell of strong black coffee percolating on the woodstove. Ah, I follow my nose down the loft stairs. I'm met by Mindy and Matt talking with their heads together in an intense conversation. I shrug my apologies that I am interrupting and head for the mugs and cream. Matt smiles at my PJs that consist of his oversize t-shirt as I had not packed any and I blush. I should've thought to change first. Oh well, nothing a big cozy blanket can't fix once I am caffeinated. All I want is to be cozy by the fire and read the Bible that I notice lying on the coffee table.

Mindy asks, "How was your night through the storm? Did you manage to sleep soundly?"

"Well, it was off and on but nothing to worry about," I reply.

"Thanks for keeping the fire going," Matt comments. "We both slept through it all."

"I'm grateful. You need your rest to recuperate fully and be mentally alert."

It's still dark out, so we're eagerly looking forward to sunrise and hopefully calmer seas than last night. I've always had great respect for the power of the ocean. I've been on a boat during storms and felt like a bobble being tossed to and fro with waves towering on every side. It's not my favorite place to be. I get seasick and do not escape the retching this can induce. You feel so miserable that you'd like someone to knock you out so you don't have to endure the torturous illness. Hopefully, today is not that kind of day.

It's funny that the exact spot I open the Bible to is James 1:6, which talks about how when we ask, we must believe and not doubt, because the one who doubts is like a wave of the sea, blown and tossed by the wind. Such people should not expect to receive anything from the Lord. Their loyalty is divided between God and the world and they are unstable in everything they do. There's a rebuke and a clear warning of how unbelief can ruin our prayers. Faith goes a long way toward seeing results. I must put this into practice today. I believe for a safe passage back and seeing this all through favorably until the end. The goal is that Matt can finish this invention well with his own patent in hand so he can see others benefit from it. Whatever it is, patience is a virtue that I need to practice as well.

Off to the races. We must eat, get dressed, and head back to the farm to check on the pets and allow Matt to get back to his invention with total concentration and solitude. I did overhear enough of their debate to know that Mindy wants to involve the help of Matt's dad, and he wants to do it alone without his father's financial help or influence. I can understand both sides of that coin, but sometimes we have to humble ourselves and ask for help rather than try to preserve our stubborn pride or prove our worth. But perhaps his father would try to steal his thunder/profit. I don't know enough about his character to judge either way. Or maybe Matt doesn't want to involve anyone else, so no more harm can come to the ones he loves. I will just pray for wisdom for this whole family every step of the way and mind my own business unless my opinion is required. That's easier said than done because I'm itching to share my opinions.

Mindy makes sure Matt's wound is healing nicely with no sign of infection. Once she is satisfied, she gives him a tender hug and promises to come back and check in on him with groceries in eight days. He reaches out to give me a hug which seems to communicate his thankfulness and tugs on my soul with its heartfulness. You can always tell the difference between a real hug and an obligatory hug. This is not the latter, and I take a moment to reciprocate with a hug from my soul that he seems to drink in as well.

I tell him about the satellite phone in case of an emergency and nonchalantly say over my shoulder, "See you in a week."

The sun has risen and the waves are choppy but navigable as we commence our return trip. I let Mindy drive once we're past the worst of the chop, and she is gleefully gunning it even after hearing my pleas to slow down. Wild girl! She eventually complies as the impact of the boat hitting the waves makes it quite rough and loud. As we near the marina, I take over, docking it properly in the slip, because there is always the danger of clipping another docked boat. I breathe a sigh of relief that all has gone well without any mishap. I hide the key where it belongs, tie up the boat securely, unload, and off we go to the farm to check on everything.

As we drive along the coast, all the memories of the past week start to roll over me. I feel exhausted by the emotional overload. Mindy is also unusually pensive. We're unprepared for the sight that meets our eyes as I round the last bend to the farm. A huge cedar had fallen across my driveway and hit my fence, but thankfully, it missed the house and the shed. Brian and Liam are busily chopping it up with chainsaws whirring away, and don't hear or see us approaching. I am trying to formulate an explanation for my absence, looking around for any other storm damage caused by the wind. I'm also hoping to see Bozer running around.

Finally, they glance up. They both immediately put down their saws and half run-walk to the truck with grim expressions bordering on anger and worry. I try on my sweetest smile for size.

I roll down my window and hurriedly say, "Thank you for checking on me and for helping to clean up the mess. Please help yourselves to any firewood."

"Where the heck have you been?" Brian sputters. "We've been worried sick when you weren't answering your phone. We called the school only to find out you had taken the day off, which you rarely do. There was no trace of you here, not even a note. I was thinking the worst, that somehow Daniel escaped and had gotten to you!"

Liam tries to smooth things over by saying, "We need to know your whereabouts so we can communicate and update you on the case, but also to keep you safe."

His brown eyes are studying me for any clues as to my absence, and I feign innocence by explaining that we needed some time off from all the drama and didn't even think to inform them.

"Sorry guys for any extra worry. How about you come in for a break? I can whip up some hot coffee and treats, then you can fill me in on any new happenings with the case."

I can tell they've been working for a few hours from their sweaty, wet chests and backs and could use a breather. They agree that a break sounds good, but they promise to make a path for my truck before daylight runs out.

The men help us over the big cedar, and I take a big sniff to appreciate the cedar smell that is wafting in the air.

"I can't wait to smell these logs burning in my outdoor firepit, and maybe I can make something like a cutting board out of this beautiful wood," I remark appreciatively.

A person could make a lot of money just by selling the wood, which I might consider after I keep what I want and give some away.

I call for Bozer, thinking it strange that he wasn't with the boys. He does hate the noise of loud saws. I am beginning to regret not taking him with us on the boat. I was just about to ask if the boys saw him when I hear a whimper coming from under a tall spruce tree. I rush over and I'm horrified to see that a branch the size of my thigh has fallen and pinned Bozer's back leg, preventing him from any movement. My poor pooch!

Brian has worked enough with animals to know how to create a makeshift splint with a stick and tensor bandage, so he offers his services. Meanwhile, Liam lifts the branch while I comfort Bozer and try to keep him still, so he doesn't inflict more pain with his exuberance to see me.

Mindy runs to get a bandage, and Brian hunts for the appropriate stick that will support his leg. I can see that it is a clean break and should heal nicely if we can keep him off the leg.

I feel terrible for leaving him. I can imagine how scared he was with the chain saws buzzing and not being able to go hide in the house. In addition to the pain in his leg, I wonder how long he's been pinned here? It could've been since the wee hours of the morning. Who knows?

After Brian sets his leg to his satisfaction, Liam offers to carry him into the house. I warm up some broth to add to his dog food, and he hungrily scarfs it down. I can just picture him trying to hobble on three legs to go outside through the doggy door. That could present a challenge.

Mindy is busily making coffee and defrosting coffee cake, which I had in the freezer for times like this. Daisy and her kittens seem fine and none the worse for wear. They can take care of themselves for the most part with my special cat feeder that I can fill with a week's worth of food. But I can see they've been up to some mischief with toilet paper lying around and my shredded slippers being used for tug of war. I will be finding them forever homes in a couple of weeks so I must remember to advertise at church, school, and the post office. I've grown quite attached to them but I can't keep them all. However, the tabby with green eyes may have to stay as she is my favorite.

Now that Bozer is settled in his comfy dog bed, I turn my attention to the guys. "Alright, so fill me in on what you found out about Daniel."

They exchange glances, fidget in their chairs, and finally look me in the eye. "He must have friends in the department," Liam says. "They're not sharing any info and he is getting preferential treatment with fancy meals, so it doesn't look too good."

"He held us at gunpoint, and he was going to try to get information from us by force," I say, clearly upset. "Isn't he going on trial for false imprisonment?"

Liam nods that a trial may be forthcoming, but the facts will probably be misconstrued. Unless we get Judge Mcardell, the truth may be buried and the outcome unfavorable. This guy seems to have connections in high places to be able to buy his way out of this mess.

Brian is trying to question me about my whereabouts again, but I hedge by offering them coffee and dessert. Mindy expertly steers the conversation to safer waters. I'm liking this teamwork, knowing someone always has my back.

Then, Liam mentions the fact that he hasn't seen Matteo today. "Is he resting and improving?"

"Yes, he is improving daily and there is no sign of infection, which we're grateful for," I offer.

I excuse myself to go to the bathroom and remember to close his bedroom door to cover our tracks. I'm not sure how long we can keep this charade up. We will need creative ideas to keep them from visiting or coming to the house this week.

The boys thank us for the treats and declare, "We'd better get back to work."

We thank them for their help and breathe sighs of relief once the door closes behind them.

Telling them the truth would be so much easier, but we're not sure who to fully trust yet. We had promised Matt to keep his whereabouts quiet for a week. He owes me big time. I don't like stretching the truth or hedging. Forgive me, Lord, I hope You understand my motives.

I forgot I was supposed to do some canning today. It's Saturday and my full day off. I really don't feel up to it, but I must push through and 'get 'er done', as my dad would say. Mindy is only too happy to help, and the English proverb, "many hands make light work," is very apropos in this case. I begin by finding all my jars, lids, recipes, vinegar, and dill as she preps all the veggies. I prefer doing batches of seven jars at a time in the pressure canner with the outcome of pickled carrots, beets, cucumbers, and beans. This process will take us most of the day, but we will reap the benefits all winter long. It's funny how I'm thinking in terms of "we" now and not just "me."

However, I shouldn't take Mindy for granted. I have no idea how long she plans on staying. My guess is until the invention is complete, delays seem to be inevitable because of the pushback. How long has this been in the works anyway? I wonder. What better time to get answers than when two women are bonding in the kitchen?

"So, Mindy." She looks at me. "How long has Matt been working on this particular invention?"

She smiles knowingly, calculates in her head, and responds, "The idea was birthed nine years ago but has been seven years in the making, I figure."

"What is it about this area that he needs to complete his project?"

"Well now, I cannot divulge that secret quite yet. I will leave it to Matt to explain when the time is right."

Drat! Still no clues. I might have to try and get my hands on her little red book full of notes that she keeps in her purse. But then that would be me trying to make things happen in the flesh and not relying on God's perfect plan and timing. Not to mention that I would be betraying my new friend's trust, which is hard to gain back. It's probably not worth losing a friendship over, but it's oh so tempting to do things my way. Time to say no to the flesh and submit to God's way.

My phone pings with a reminder that the soul sisters want to get together tonight at Linda's, and I am to bring an appetizer. I am feeling stretched beyond my limits and figure I can send my apologies with the excuse that I have to take care of Bozer with his recent injury. I am learning to set healthy boundaries and to say no when I'm feeling overwhelmed. I can recognize that this situation qualifies as a time to rest, and I shouldn't take on too much, or I may snap. Then, what good am I to others or even to myself? I have to remind myself of our soul sister's motto, "all is well, all is well," especially when life feels like we're surviving instead of thriving. At times, a little reminder is all I need to switch to that mindset.

I am startled out of my musings when I hear the timer go off, signifying my jars are boiling and ready to be transferred to my counter, where I will eagerly wait for the pop of every jar as it seals. Then I am certain that each jar has passed the preservation test and is safe to store.

Fun fact: The process of canning was invented by Nicholas Appert of France in 1809 in response to a call from his government to preserve food for the army and navy (Britannica.com). I get to enjoy the benefits to this day. Thank you, Nicholas.

"Thanks for your help, Mindy." I smile at her. "It took half the time usually required from start to finish."

"Oh Marina, you are a joy to work with and I am just so grateful that you took us in. You just keep helping us with no concern for your own safety. You could've walked away and gone back to your normal life, but instead, you took a chance on us. We appreciate you."

I give her a hug and exclaim, "Let's celebrate our friendship and our canning success today by rewarding ourselves with a soak in the hot tub under the stars tonight."

She readily agrees. We notice that the boys have finished clearing the driveway and are moving my truck back to the house. They amble towards the hot tub to say good night and we thank them for their amazing help.

"We will be sure to stop by and bring you a few jars of our canning today as appreciation for pitching in to help us damsels in distress," I say to them.

Being bachelors, they're both delighted at the sound of that and wish us a good soak. I would invite them to join us, but I don't really want their sweaty bodies sharing our same water. I wish to keep this a girl's night and not to have to watch every word I say. See, I am improving daily on setting boundaries and saying no. I am learning not to care what people think or to try to please them at the expense of my own sanity.

CHAPTER TEN

I do not take my eight hours of uninterrupted sleep for granted. I know many of my friends comment on how sleep is a struggle. I am blessed with the uncanny ability to fall asleep as soon as my head hits the pillow, just like my dad. I hope Matt is getting some rest and not working around the clock. I can't believe I'm already looking forward to checking in on him. I suppose I have to admit to myself that I miss him just a wee bit.

As I enter the kitchen, I am reminded of our labor of love as twenty-eight colorful jars greet my eyes with their beautiful display. The sight brings a smile to my lips and all the memories of family time spent with my mom and sisters in the kitchen canning every fall come rushing back. In addition, Mom would add canned peaches, pears, saskatoons, and cherries to that list. I happily start carting them to my cold room and set a few aside as gifts as I promised. I practically trip over a kitten that has climbed out of her box and try not to let a swearword roll out as I narrowly miss dropping a jar onto her little head. Oh, that could've spelled disaster in so many ways. It felt as though a hand held me up so I wouldn't fall. Thank you, God.

I check on Bozer, who is still favoring his good leg, and debate on whether to take him to the vet. All they would do is put a cast on his leg, which he would probably chew off anyways. I trust Brian's skills and just want to make sure Bozer heals properly, so I bring him an extra blanket to cushion his leg.

I am sensing that today is a good day to introduce Mindy to my cousins, and perhaps a total change of plans will do us good. I enjoy being spontaneous and think it's time to plan an enjoyable outing. To my surprise, Mindy is not on my wavelength and wants a down day to rest at home. Although that sounds tempting, I have ulterior motives and mention that they have horses and that the day might involve going horseback riding on the beach. Nope, the offer doesn't budge her stance to take care of Bozer and snuggle the kittens, so I set off to enjoy the gorgeous sunny day on my own.

My cousins all farm together, share their equipment and help each other through harvest season, and I like to pitch in whenever I can. The forty-five-minute drive is peaceful and my time to sing, pour out my thoughts to God and feel His strength, presence, and love begin to fill me up. I've received many songs, lyrics, and melodies while driving, and I've discovered it's my creative zone. Today is no exception, so I press my voice recorder button as I break out in song,

"We've never been this way before
Walk through the open door
Believe by faith and trust in the One who saves us
Love like a river is flowing from the throne
So deep, so wide, so high
I can hardly contain it, oh
Embrace it, run with it, give it away
It's the only way, oh."

I am so overcome by His love, which casts out all fear. I realize that love wins every single time because Jesus is love. I once heard a prophet by the name of Bob Jones say, "When you get to heaven, the only question you'll need to answer is, have you learned to love?" The reason he knew this was because he died and went to heaven and was asked that very question but was given the choice to come back and tell us. Profound. I guess that's why God gave us free will so we could choose to love, to accept His most precious gift of love, namely Jesus, so we could be reunited back to Him where we came from and where we belong. I feel another song coming, so I hit the record button again. Our choices do matter, and I want to choose His ways over those of the world. I pray for truth to win and justice to be served, but if I don't see it happen on this side of eternity, I know who gets the last word.

I see the ranch coming into view and marvel at how well-maintained the fences are. Everything looks like it's running in pristine condition. I know all the work that goes on behind the scenes and I'm looking forward to seeing everyone and catching up on all the news. I didn't call ahead, so we shall see who's home for my surprise visit. The horses are grazing, their sleek coats glistening in the sunshine, and I hope to ride Aleta, a sleek chestnut mare that I've bonded with since she was a foal.

The maples lining the drive are boasting their beautiful reds, and I still see pumpkins in the garden ready to be brought in. Their gorgeous rock home is bustling with activity as the eight-year-old twins, Al, and Ali, come bursting out to give me a hug before I even have the chance to knock.

"Hi, my favorite twins. I see I can't sneak up and surprise you two!"

They laugh and pull me inside to show off their catch to Rebecca, their petite mom, who is elbow-deep in flour, making a fresh batch of bread.

"Oh, hi Marina, so glad to see you're OK. What a nice surprise! You're just in time to help me knead some dough if you like. We have so much to catch up on. You have a lot of explaining to do from the stories we heard this past week!"

She gives me a big bear hug, staining me with flour. I gladly grab an apron and proceed to tell her about my action-packed week, minus some details that might send her into protective mama bear mode. The twins run around, chasing each other. She sends them outside to go help the boys with their chores.

Rebecca is aghast at what this Daniel is capable of and declares that justice has to be forthcoming, or she will get our lawyer cousin involved. But she also wants all the juicy information on this new Matteo guy, who sounds like a dreamy catch. I assure her we're just friends. I haven't known him for very long, but she stresses that those were intense days of fellowship fraught with danger, overcoming obstacles and triumphing together. She's always been such a romantic at heart and did get her dreamy guy in Bo, who adores her. We form our dough blobs into pans and cover them with a cloth to allow them to rise. We then take ourselves outside to go see the boys and those horses.

I spot Ben, my strapping sixteen-year-old second cousin, mucking out the stalls. I wave while walking towards Bo, who is in the round pen training a new horse. I love to see how patiently he walks through the paces until he is satisfied with the results.

He casually strolls over and looks me up and down to make sure I'm in one piece. "You look OK. Heard you got involved with some shady characters," he smirks. "Did you win?"

Rebecca hits his arm, and I smile that all is well in my neck of the woods, knowing that he will get all the details out of her later.

"Good. Are you ready to go for a ride on the beach? The tide is out and I think a couple of the horses need to stretch their legs," he grins, "you could probably use a little exercise yourself."

Oh, cousins and teasing go hand in hand. I plan to give him a good dose of his own medicine.

"Yes, I would love to pound the surf with my favorite beauty," I saucily toss back, but he is having none of it.

"Nope, Aleta already exercised today. You get to bring out Taffy, who might be a little temperamental, but that should match up with you nicely."

It's my turn to punch him on the shoulder and go in search of Miss Bossy. Rebecca would love to join, but she has to keep the twins busy. I suggest we each take a twin and ride double, which didn't take much convincing to twist her arm.

Off to the beach we go! Ali is hanging onto me quite tightly since she doesn't always trust me on a horse. I'm being cautious, instructing Taffy to walk, trot and then canter as she warms up. I restrain myself from going into a full gallop because of my precious passenger, but I am tempted to fly like the wind.

Rebecca is taking it more slowly, so I slow my pace to enjoy the countryside. The next stretch will take us through my favorite forest, with towering cedars, green ferns, and deciduous trees covered in moss. Then, it opens up onto the sandy beach, where the horses love to gallop up and down. Aleta loves to prance in the waves, but I am guessing Taffy might be more skittish about the water. By her reaction, I can tell I guessed correctly. I sense the twins want to run and explore the beach, so we let them hop off. This gives me the perfect opportunity to let Taffy run. I love the feeling of flying with the wind in my hair and the total sense of freedom. Too late. Suddenly, I spot a sea lion sunning itself on the rocks. This spooks Taffy, who stops suddenly and sends me flying over her head into the sand. I land on my back and the wind is knocked out of me. Oomph! So much for freedom! I check for any damage, check on Taffy, and see Rebecca trotting over with an alarmed look on her face.

"What spooked her? Are you okay, Marina? You had some good air time. Can you breathe?"

"Yep, I'm good. That sea lion set her off and I just went for a spill. Guess I will take it easy from now on."

We hop back on to go check on the twins down the beach, and I slow down to enjoy the sun on the waves that sparkle like diamonds.

"You know, you're lucky you didn't break a leg or hit your head on that rock that was a few inches away," counters Rebecca.

"Yeah, my angels work overtime to protect me," I say. "I thank God for that. I don't have time for more broken bones at the moment. Bozer's leg is enough to worry about for now."

That comment launches us into how Mindy is doing, and before we know it, the twins hop back on, and we're ready to head back before it gets too dark. The sunset is just starting to cast its pinks across the horizon and I revel in the beauty as we trot up the drive. I know I'm going to get teased for my little soaring moment, but maybe Rebecca won't mention anything to Bo and it will be our shared secret. I had no such luck. She can't resist telling her side of the story as we brush down the horses, and even Ben is joining in on the fun. They're a bunch of traitors, but I wouldn't trade my family for anything. We have each other's backs no matter what. We spend the rest of the evening enjoying delicious homemade bread with a variety of toppings and sharing our ideas, dreams, and hopes for the ranch, my predicament, and life in general.

I leave feeling refreshed and ready to tackle whatever life throws my way. Rather than waiting for things to happen, I will act and live my life to the fullest by using the passions, talents, and gifts given to me by a loving Creator. I want to create, not just react, which is how I've been living this past week. It is time to take the bull by the horns and not live in fear of what Daniel might do next or what he might get away with. Instead, I will live fully despite what he can do to us. I must not focus on what-ifs but on what is possible. All things are possible, and I believe that Matt can finish what he started no matter the pushback. It's weird how his dream has become a part of mine, and I want to help him fulfill it, even if I don't know exactly what it is yet.

Mindy looks like she had a relaxing day herself and enjoyed every minute of it. She is beaming, and there's a new sparkle to her eyes of renewed energy to match mine. We share our day over some hot apple cider with cinnamon sticks. She opens up about her past losses, victories, and dreams for her own future. I decide we can become each other's cheerleaders and write down our goals. "Where there is no revelation, people cast off restraint; but blessed is the one who heeds wisdom's instruction" (Proverbs 29:18). I grab a yellow paper and write:

1. record an original song
2. finish a painting
3. publish my novel
4. help others see their potential and reach their goals; and
5. find my soul mate

Then, I put it on the fridge where I can see it every day to remind me where I am going.

CHAPTER ELEVEN

I awaken from a troubling dream where I'm always on the run. In the dream, I can't seem to shake my pursuer, and a wolf is always stalking me. The second I think I had escaped the man's clutches, I see the wolf's eyes glowing through the trees and I can't help but think this is related to Matt. I wonder if he's run into more trouble and if he needs our help. I cover him in prayer, then get up to make breakfast before I start my workday.

Bozer greets me with a yip from his bed. I check his leg and it seems to be holding up, so I feed him and carry him outside so he doesn't have to maneuver the doggie door awkwardly. The sunrise is coming up over the trees with pink hues as I spot two eagles circling above, hoping to spot their breakfast, so I check to make sure the kittens are safe inside and haven't escaped. All is well, and I sense God's peace wash over me. I thank Him for giving me one more day to live for Him, one more day to draw breath and make a positive difference. I ask for His grace and wisdom to recognize each opportunity and not squander any chances away by living with blinders on but be alive to aid those around me.

Mindy is already puttering in the kitchen, so I share my dream with her. She wonders if we should check in on him sooner rather than wait until Friday. Perhaps I can sneak away Tuesday after I teach since it's a short day and I only have to be there for two hours. She is relieved that we can leave sooner and she promises to shop for supplies to take with us. I am excited to see his progress. I hope all is well, and we have nothing to be worried about.

My teaching day flies by quickly, with Linda checking in. They missed me at soul sisters. I tell her that all is well. Bozer is on the mend as well as Matt, and I've prioritized my goals to finish my projects. She is proud of me and cheering me on to finish as she can't wait to read my book, see my painting, and listen to my song.

I hug her. "How's Carl, your dream boyfriend, doing?"

"Well, we hit a bit of a snag," she said sadly. "We seem to be getting too serious too fast, so we decided to cool it a bit and take a break for a couple of weeks."

"What! I had no idea. I mean, everything looked like it was going so perfectly. I'm sorry for judging from the outside and not lending you my support. I can't really offer advice as I have no dating experience, but I can listen anytime you need a sounding board."

"Thanks, I just might take you up on that offer because it's so hard to keep my distance right now, even though I agreed with his plan. But I guess it's a good time to journal and get in touch with God to help me process my feelings."

"You are amazing. I know you both will come out of this stronger, having learned more about yourselves in the process. I know it's hard all the same though."

We hug again, and I say goodbye, feeling sorry I can't help more concretely. Sometimes I want to rescue my friends from their pain, but I realize that going through it is part of life, growth, and development. She will come through this wall on the other side having learned about patience, trust, and surrender, and being able to help others through their similar pain. The very thing that we struggle with in life and overcome becomes our badge of honor. We then have the authority to help and speak into other people's lives, and it becomes our shining testimony. I love that what the enemy wants to harm us with, God turns around and uses it for not only our good but for the whole world that will listen. That is powerful and so redeeming. The enemy thought he had won when Jesus was crucified, but it was the greatest victory over darkness this world will ever see! Jesus suffered for us all so that we could be rescued from evil and be reunited with God. When Jesus returns, His victory will be complete! He gets the last word. I feel fired up and like I want to go rescue Matt tonight. But maybe God's got this, and I'd better stick to plan B. It's not good to get ahead of Him and I should just wait until tomorrow as planned.

The drive home is soothing and melodious as I sing my heart out whilst enjoying the ocean view. I glimpse a black bear with her cub and marvel at their thick rippling fur. They don't have to hibernate here yet as it hasn't gotten very cold, so they're out foraging and enjoying the sunshine. I can't help but pull over and take a few pictures. The cub is like a round puff ball, climbing over logs, playing alongside its mama, oblivious to any danger, while the mama bear is on the lookout. Pictures can never quite capture the beauty because it's so far away and I don't have a fancy lens, but it's fun to try.

I get home to see Mindy humming away while packing all the supplies in the totes. I load them up to keep them out of sight in case we get unexpected visitors. My canopy is already on the truck for the winter to keep the rain off anything I might be carting. Tonight, I feel like eating in style with some steak and grilled vegetables with balsamic vinegar. I am trying to keep the carbs and sugars on the down-low, so no potatoes or dessert for me tonight. Mindy has decided to follow suit to make it easier for meal prep and to maximize her energy. We want to be at our best to face whatever awaits us tomorrow.

I might even pack my Glock tomorrow for self-defense. A girl must be wise and prepared at all times. My dad taught me how to shoot, so I'm a pretty good markswoman, and I bet Mindy knows how to hit a target too. She raises an eyebrow when she sees me packing it and then shrugs and nods that it might not be a bad idea after all. That's my girl. I might even throw in a BB gun for good measure, so we each have something to aim for. Mindy laughs outright when I bring that out of the closet, but from a distance, we can both be intimidating. Now that we have our bases covered, it's time to feast.

We make quick work of barbequing the steaks to medium-rare and grilling our veggies to perfection. I take out my best china, steak knives, wine glasses, and candlelight to enjoy the moment. I ask Mindy about her love life. I'm sure she had her fair share of interests over the years.

"Yes, there were a few men who tried to catch my attention, but my heart will always be with my teen crush who got away. We were both young and foolish, and I guess I played too hard to get. He ended up dating my cousin and marrying her five years later."

"What? How awful! You had to watch from the sidelines and be happy for them, even though you were heartbroken."

"I was happy for them and figured it was not meant to be for me," she says. "I am content being single. I have no strings attached, so I have total freedom to be here, for example, and be independent."

"I admire you for your tenacity and zest for life," I say. "I am content as well, and maybe that will be my lot in life; happily single and serving God with pure devotion and passion."

"Maybe," she replies with a sly smile, "but don't miss the opportunity for love or close yourself off to it in case it is what God has planned for you."

"Touché, it doesn't hurt to be open to all the possibilities God brings my way."

The moon is practically full. It bathes the landscape in a serene glow that takes my breath away. Time to enjoy the view from the hot tub. I feel so spoiled every time I jump into the bubbles as I know this is an added luxury, but I feel it is important for my well-being. It's worth every penny in my mind.

CHAPTER TWELVE

The next day, I still need to go to work in the morning before embarking on our next check-in, which is starting to feel urgent. I manage to talk with Linda, hedging a little, about my plans for the day. I teach my four students, who are actually getting quite good because they're practicing, which makes me happy, and we head home on the double. Mindy is waiting for me with the keys in one hand and a lunch bag in the other. I run in and change, and we are off to the races. She is looking forward to driving the boat, and I might just let her, as I need to eat and mentally prepare for whatever lies ahead. We discuss our options of stealth and possibly splitting up once we get to the island, each with our weapon in case of an emergency or an encounter with a questionable character.

The loading of the totes goes without a hitch, and we settle in for the forty-five-minute ride on choppy seas. The salty cold spray of the waves is enough to cool us down and make us want to keep our hoods on. I spot an otter swimming on its back happily munching on some sea delicacy and can hear the loons warbling their cry as we near the island. I scan the embankment and see no signs of anyone. I still see smoke coming from the chimney, and no other boat is moored at the dock. I motion for her to kill the engine as soon as we're near enough to tie off. We stash the totes in the trees so we can go scout the rear and front of the cabin first. I show her which trail to take while I scramble up the left side, praying we're not too late. All seems quiet, but I notice a black truck parked down the trail. It looked like somebody stashed it to enter on foot and with stealth. So, despite our best efforts, someone else found out where Matt was hiding. I guess it shouldn't surprise me with all the fancy surveillance technology that is available nowadays that someone was able to track him down.

I hope Mindy is in position on the back side of the cabin, as I am ready to burst in from the front side. Strange, I see two burly dudes walking out the front door in broad daylight with angry expressions on their faces. Truth be told, they look disappointed and are scratching their heads. I hide further back in the trees in a crouching position, knowing my dark clothes should be camouflaged against the tree trunks. True to form, they look around, hop in the black truck, rev the engine, and roar away. I wait for a few minutes, but it really feels like a lifetime, and I slowly tiptoe to the front window and peer in. Things have been upturned, thrown around, and emptied, but there is no sign of Matt. I cautiously enter with the gun leading the way in my shaking hands, just in case they left someone behind. Mindy has entered from the back and done a search of the main level, signaling with her head that the coast is clear. I creep up the stairs to the loft and cannot find any sign of Matt. I call out his name so that if he is hiding, he will know it's safe to come out now. I hear a thump over my head and realize there is an attic door I never noticed before in the closet. Upon closer inspection, I see a slightly open hatch and a pair of anxious eyes peering out.

"Matt, is that you? Are you alright? How did you get up there? It's OK, you can come down. The two burly guys left. It's just Mindy and myself here now."

He hesitantly opens the door and looks so relieved to see me that he leaps down like a cat and gives me a huge hug.

"How did you know to come? Are you sure there is no one else lurking around? You're holding a gun! Is Aunt Mindy safe?"

By this time, Mindy appears in the closet doorway, looking relieved to see her nephew in one piece. She hugs him fiercely while blubbering away on his sleeve and exclaiming, "Brilliant, you had time to scale up there while two guys wreaked havoc down here and left with nothing to show for it. Where do you have everything hidden? Thank the good Lord you're safe!"

We all burst out laughing as the emotions are running high and we all want to get our questions answered at the same time. We start by climbing back down to the kitchen to make some tea, picking up the chairs, and gathering around the table with the curtains drawn. We don't feel very safe anymore from prying eyes, and I wonder if they'll want to come back later tonight. I think it's best to keep changing locations, but I'd rather just face them head-on so we don't have to hide anymore. We begin by filling Matt in on how I had a warning dream and how we listened to our intuition to come to check on him sooner.

"I'm so glad that you paid attention to your premonition. I could've been holed up there for a lot longer knowing I had no backup. Tell me all the details you remember about the truck and describe the guys you saw."

As I launch into all the specifics, Matt begins to take notes and tries to draw the men. Now, we want to hear his side of the story.

"Well, I knew that Daniel would probably send more thugs my way, hoping to get his hands on my blueprints, formula, and notes. So, I jimmy-rigged a hunting camera to my computer so I could detect if anyone came down the trail. I worked around the clock, which allowed me to finish my main calculations. I've also been in close contact with the doctors and colleagues that I've been working with over the last several months to finalize the specifications. I sent samples to the lab via helicopter, which might've tipped my location to the bad guys. I made sure to hide all evidence by encrypting all my files and sending digital copies to the lab, which has high security in place. I had stored my laptop and files in a safe in the attic but knew time was of the essence, so I sent the completed files with my most trusted man on the helicopter. It might be a good idea to clean up here and get back to your place before dark, as those thugs will come back. They might assume that I was on the helicopter, but if they see lights on, it won't bode well for us."

I don't need any more motivation. I jump into action, sweeping up the debris and getting ready to hightail it out of there. I guess we won't need those extra supplies after all and will just have to reload them onto the boat. I peer out to make sure we're still alone, while Matt grabs his belongings and Mindy secures the place. I feel like we are still in a mission impossible real-life scenario and keep my gun handy as we hurry down to the boat. Everything looks untouched, which is a good thing. I let Matt drive so I can keep a lookout with my binoculars.

The wind is still gusty, and now we're fighting the waves, which will slow us down but can't be helped. I am debating going a different route when I glimpse a speed boat gaining on us from the west side of the island. Drats, they must've been hiding in the next cove over. I see a drone flying overhead. I feel like shooting it down, but I don't want to waste my bullets. Mindy grabs her BB gun and does it for me. It's nice to know she's a good shot. She smiles saucily, and I motion for her to keep praying. We're not in the clear yet. I know these islands very well, so I hand the gun to Matt and grab the wheel, hoping that I will choose the best cove to hide our boat in. I am banking on the fact that darkness will be our friend soon. There seems to be a fog rolling in, which will also aid us tonight. Our prayers seem to be working. Thank you, God.

I see a series of inlets and choose the middle arm to go down. It has many places to hide and take cover. This boat only needs one foot of water to float, so I can bring it into the shallows with no fear of hitting the bottom. Unless the tide changes, we should be good for a few hours sheltered by a huge rock outcropping. I throw the anchor overboard to keep us in one spot and open the tote labeled food to make us a simple supper. Croissants with cold cuts, gouda cheese, lettuce, and pickles make our waiting time worthwhile. We're careful not to light any lanterns or speak loudly, as water carries sound so easily. The temperature is dropping, so I pull out some wool blankets and we hunker down ready to wait this out.

I am hoping they went down the first arm. With night setting in, they might choose to call it quits for the night but I'm not willing to take a chance yet. I listen for any sounds of a running motor while getting sleepy. The stars are so beautiful, and it feels like I can reach out and touch them. The cuddy cabin with the bed is calling my name, but I urge Mindy and Matt to go lay down out of the elements for an hour to relax. There's no use in all of us keeping watch. We might as well take shifts and get some rest. They agree, and Matt offers to take the second watch.

I am awakened abruptly by someone shaking me. I gasp and jump, hitting my head on the side of the boat. So much for my attempt at being alert and keeping watch. I hope I get it right for when it really counts, and Jesus comes back looking for those who are watching and ready. It reminds me of the ten virgins spoken of in Matthew 25, where five are ready with extra oil for their lamps and five ran out of oil. They all fell asleep which I can relate to. Only those who had extra oil could trim their lamps. While the five foolish virgins were gone buying more oil, the bridegroom came at midnight and welcomed the five wise virgins into the wedding banquet, then closed the door. The five virgins returned and asked for the door to be opened, but he claimed he did not know them. The warning is that we should keep watch because we do not know the day or the hour and must be ready at all times. To me, the oil signifies spending time with Jesus; soaking in His Word, praying, and worshipping him with my life as my best friend so that He knows me. It always comes down to the relationship, period. I come out of my daze by Matt's hand waving in front of my nose, and I acknowledge that it is his turn to keep watch, while I gratefully slide into the warm spot he just vacated below deck beside a snoring Mindy. He chuckles at my incoherent ways and resumes my spot for one more hour.

I continue dreaming about being ready and not wanting to miss the train. I'm always being chased and have to fight to get close enough to hop on the train before it leaves without me. I guess this message is too important to ignore and one I must guard and fight for. I peek my head out and notice that we better get moving or we will be high centered and caught in a low tide. If that happens, we will have to wait for hours until the high tide comes back. Not wanting to be a sitting duck, I climb out, but to my dismay, we are already grounded. Good thing it is a sandy bottom. I hurriedly roll my pants up, take my socks and shoes off, and jump overboard into ankle-deep water. Matt is looking at me in consternation, while I grab the rope and start to pull the boat to deeper waters. It is freezing water and I hate cold water as it gives me a brain freeze. I pull and slosh through as fast as I can, which is pretty sluggish. I'm triumphant when I reach one foot of water, throw the anchor in, and climb aboard to Mindy, who had the forethought to get me a towel and is rubbing my feet and legs to get feeling back into them. Matt has started the engine and we're slowly making our way back through the inlet to the open ocean and, hopefully, to the marina without being detected. We need favor on our side tonight.

I keep watch behind us for any sign of movement or the sound of another motor gaining on us, but all is peaceful. We still have a half-hour boat ride to reach the marina and have to use our lights to see any logs or debris in our way, which is Mindy's job as the lookout scout. Teamwork is needed with all hands on deck. I have time to think if I want to lead them to my doorway again or drop off Matt at Brian's until this all blows over and those two guys are caught. Wisdom and discernment are needed every step of the way.

I am overjoyed when I can see the lights from a distance. We are close and I am looking forward to a hot drink and my bed. We arrive with no incident, unload, and I take Matt home as I don't want to wake up Brian at this late hour. We're grateful that we have escaped unscathed and can regroup tomorrow. I am not a night owl, and so I make a point of not making any major decisions at night when things look so grim. The morning always brings with it new mercies, grace, and a fresh outlook on life.

Matt seems to thrive at night, so I let him drive the truck home. While he and Mindy are in a deep, whispered conversation, I find myself lulled to sleep in minutes. My head is resting on Matt's shoulder when we arrive, and he tweaks my nose, teasing me about my ability to sleep anywhere.

"Hey, it's a blessing in disguise and one that I appreciate at times like these," I retort back.

"I'm not going to carry you in though. That's where I draw the line," he cheekily responds.

"I can take care of myself," I reply mockingly. "Besides, we have totes to carry in, so let's all pull our weight."

"You two!" Mindy reprimands. "Quit your shenanigans. I want my bed too, so more work and less talk."

It feels like family already. I can get used to this. Living alone is losing its charm. We unpack in record time. I boil some water for hot apple cider and check on Bozer, who seems to be healing well and is thrilled to see us. The sleeping kittens wake up as soon as we come in. They're excited to play, so I indulge them with a string.

I sip my drink while going over our adventures with my house guests, and we marvel at how close these dangerous missions have strengthened our bonds of friendship in such a short time. We call it a night and pray for protection while we sleep.

CHAPTER THIRTEEN

Wednesday dawns with overcast skies. It looks like we're in for some heavy rain, which makes me want to read a book by the fireplace. But work duty is calling, and I can't let my students down. I get ready for my day quietly as my guests are still sleeping from our harrowing escape the night before. I boil water for oatmeal with apples, raisins, cinnamon, and maple syrup just like my dad used to make it. It's funny how some foods and smells take you right back to your childhood memories. I love it when I dream of him because it's so good to see him again and it feels like a gift.

When I get to work, Liam is waiting for me in the parking lot with a frustrated look on his face. Oh dear, I may have been found out. I go to roll down my window, but he is having none of it and jumps in the front seat.

"What in the world do you think you're doing, going on dangerous escapades that could threaten my investigation?" He gruffly demands.

"Good morning to you too!" I respond. "I'm sorry for not keeping you in the loop. Matt wanted one week of secrecy to finish his project, and I granted it to him."

"Well, I was following those two guys, which led me to you on the island where I was close to catching them, but then they took off after you in the boat before I had a chance to bring them in, and now they've vanished again. I was worried for your safety all night!"

"Again, I truly am sorry for causing you any worry and will try to include you in any future plans."

"You are not to try anything new. These thugs are nothing to trifle with. They will not hesitate to kill to get what they want. Daniel's trial is this Friday, so I will prep you for testifying and have a lawyer friend ready to go with the report. Brian and I have been working hard behind the scenes to get this all ready.

"I am on your side," he says softly. "Please trust me and let me in, no matter what Matt tries to make you promise. I need to know the details to get my job done correctly. For your safety and his, we may have to move him to a safe house until this is all resolved and finalized."

"Thank you for all your hard work. I wouldn't know where to begin in terms of hiring a lawyer and getting the paperwork ready. I appreciate you both working on your gifts to get this done the proper way. You should let Matt know the details, as he may have connections with professional lawyers who have worked on these high-level cases before and could help foot the bill. You may have to convince him about the safe house too. I was thinking of sending him to Brian's house for now, where you could post some guys to guard the farm, but I will leave that to your expertise."

"My lawyer is good, but it might help to bring a team on board, so I will discuss this with Matt today while you're at work. Please, Marina, try to stay out of trouble for a couple of hours. Work with me here."

"Sure thing, Liam. I will be on my best behavior and toe the line, but you know I hate rules." I grin and jump out to avoid his retort, wave goodbye, and head into the school.

The school is teeming with energy and activity as Thanksgiving is just around the corner, and I notice turkey art decorating the walls with all the things the kids are thankful for. There are precious things all around to read like, I'm thankful for my new puppy. I'm thankful for my dad, who is back from his army trip. I'm thankful for my new baby brother. I'm thankful for my mom, who is making my favorite turkey dinner."

It causes me to reflect on all the things I'm thankful for, and the idea of a project begins to take shape. My students and I could put these thankful quotes into a song and record it for the parents as a thanksgiving gift. I mention my idea to a few students, and they're excited to come up with their own sayings and a melody line, which gives us focus, joy, and creativity. I get lost in the music world with them and time flies by before I notice it's time to go home and see what the boys have decided. I am so thankful that my job is something I love to do and provides an outlet for me amid all the chaos.

I get home and I'm met at the door by a solemn-looking Matt, who motions me inside to talk.

"I wish you would've given me a heads up that Liam was going to stop by and question me," Matt quirks.

"Right, I got distracted teaching and never thought to send you a text. Sorry about that. I presumed that he was just going to discuss a lawyer, the court case on Friday, and a safe house; you know, business-related stuff that you'd have a better handle on than me," I counter.

"I really wanted to keep the details under wraps for a few more days to give me time to finalize the legal complexities with my team of lawyers. Now I'm forced to speed up the process for the court hearing in two days, and I really do not want to go to a safe house. That will limit my freedom to get things done. I do understand that you are tired of being in danger's way and I do want to keep you and my aunt safe. I'm considering Brian's place, but maybe a hotel in town during the proceedings would be better for now. Liam can post a bodyguard there if he wants, I suppose."

Mindy pipes in that we should prepare our testimonies because we will all be called upon to testify and should focus our energies on being productive. I agree, grab my laptop, sniff the air appreciatively at some Thai dish that Mindy must be laboring over, and head to the living room to jot down some notes. I receive a text that Liam wants us to meet with his lawyer tomorrow to go over the details and make sure our testimonies are ready to withstand being cross-examined. Good, I can go after work. I'm looking forward to getting this over with and seeing Daniel prosecuted and justice served.

I sense a gentle prodding from the Holy Spirit that I should forgive Daniel before appearing in court, so I don't have any offense in my heart, and I can speak without bitterness. I immediately acknowledge the truth that I need to deal with this issue. So, I choose with an act of my will to forgive Daniel for trying to harm me and my friends.

"I release him and loose him from my soul, will, and emotions so that he no longer has any hold on me. It is not my job to take revenge, so I surrender my desire to see him pay and leave the outcome in Your capable hands," I say aloud.

I feel better already and sense the tension and stress leaving my body, replaced by a deep abiding peace that I know will sustain me through the trials ahead. God never said it would be easy, but that we would go through testing with Him by our side. He is always there to help us overcome, be strengthened, and give us the words needed at the right time. I will need to testify His words and not my own to win this battle.

I know Matt might be worried that sensitive information might be leaked before it's the right time and he has his patent in hand. So, I pray for him too. I might even bring up the topic of forgiveness at dinner so they, too, can be free. Forgiveness is a powerful weapon of light that releases us from the enemy's hold.

When I broach the subject during our delicious meal, Matt looks at me with disbelief, and Mindy looks a little more accommodating but still hesitant.

I elaborate, "It's a good thing to take inventory every night and forgive all who have offended or hurt you, and sometimes the hardest one to forgive is yourself. I feel it is important to forgive Daniel before the trial so we can have a clear conscience and peace about the surrendered outcome."

"I suppose you're right and I can see the logic in it, but that is so hard to do in reality," comments Matt.

"Yes, sometimes you just have to say the words out loud, and your heart will catch up eventually. The crucial step is to acknowledge your hurt, bring it to the cross and let Jesus take it from you," I admit.

Mindy bursts into tears and shares how she needed the reminder because her heart was starting to feel like a hardened heart, just like it is mentioned in Ezekiel 36:26 where God says he will give us a new heart, remove our heart of stone and give us a heart of flesh. I give her a hug and pray that verse over her as she repents out loud for holding grievances against Daniel and the other men. After she finishes blowing her nose, her peaceful face is transformed into a serene smile that changes her whole demeanor.

"I declare I have a whole new outlook and I'm even filled with God's love for Daniel. I'm so amazed by this total switch. I sure needed this fresh outlook. Thank you, Marina," Mindy gushes.

"I was just being obedient to what He showed me, and now I want His love for Daniel too," I exclaim.

Matt chuckles at our exuberance. "You both sound lovey-dovey, but I will have to process this on my own tonight in my own way."

"Fair enough, I can't wait to see your shining face in the morning," I reply.

Mindy and I sing our way through the dishes and marvel at the lightheartedness that has replaced the fears and worries we previously had about the case.

CHAPTER FOURTEEN

I jump out of bed, ready to tackle a new day with a clean slate. I feel fifteen pounds lighter and have a new zest for life. It's amazing what forgiveness can do. I bump into Matt in the hall downstairs and can't quite make out his face in the dark, so I switch the light on.

"Hey, what are you doing so early in the morning putting bright lights on?" asks Matt squintingly.

I laugh and peer at his face to see if I can see it shining with a new inner peace. "Just checking to see if you prayed successfully last night. I think I see fewer worry lines. Do you feel lighter, like a burden has lifted from off your shoulders?" I ask.

"I suppose so," he says. "I can tell you over breakfast. Just let me get to the bathroom first please."

"Sure thing. Can't wait to hear all about it," I perkily say as I flounce past him.

I start on scrambled eggs, sausage, and toast while the coffee is brewing, whistling a joyful tune. Mindy joins in, and I turn to give her a morning hug as she reiterates feeling like a brand-new person inside too.

Matt starts setting the table and states, "I can finally understand you women going on about feeling God's love because last night I asked Him to forgive me. I opened my heart to Him if He would have me. I forgave a whole list of people that He brought to mind and feel like I've been made new again."

This statement is met by us girls doing the happy dance of joy, laughing, crying, and hugging him while thanking God for this huge step taken.

He laughs and confesses, "I don't think I'm done forgiving but I know that it is a day-by-day task to keep short accounts and do a soul check. The Scripture that came to life for me was John 8:12, which talks about embracing Jesus as the light of the world and never having to walk in darkness because I have the light that leads to life."

We both exclaim how amazing that is and want to take communion to celebrate, which is like our daily medicine to bring healing to our bodies. We keep the slate clean every day by accepting Jesus' blood to purify us and set us in right standing with God. The meal is consumed in a celebratory party marked with joyful faces all around.

I gasp when I see the time and have to leave for work pronto or I will be late. I revel in the beauty of the fall colors during my drive, but I notice some are starting to fall already. The students are excited to continue working on their songs of thanksgiving and I offer a few tips on melody lines and words, but overall, they have the right idea. I don't have time to linger to chat with my colleagues as the lawyer will be expecting me.

I rush over, grab my notes, and see that Liam has already arrived, which doesn't surprise me as he is very punctual. He introduces me to his friend, and we get right down to business. His friend hands me some files and asks me some questions to verify the details of that dreadful day we were hijacked. He tells me that my preliminary hearing tomorrow is just to see if there is enough evidence for a trial. The trial will take place in a few months. He tells me to be concise, clear, stick to the facts, and just answer the questions calmly. I can do it only by the grace of God because I tend to react when I'm being badgered. I will have to be prayed up. I thank them for their time and drive home slowly trying to take it all in. I drive to the spot where it happened just to see if I can recall any details I may have forgotten and take more notes.

I thought my body might respond to the trauma of that day, but I must've really forgiven him because I don't have that knife in the gut kind of feeling. Just an awareness that something terrible could've happened here but we were spared and protected. I give thanks and sing my own spontaneous song of thankfulness for being saved and thank my angels, who, if I could see in the spirit realm, would've been shielding me. I dance over the spot in the sand to redeem it, to declare to the enemy that fear has no hold on me. God can take what was meant for evil and turn it for good. That's the awesome God that I serve.

I feel rejuvenated and head home to tell the others the good news. I forgot they're probably at the lawyer's getting their instructions. I actually have the house to myself, which hasn't happened in a while. I call my mom and sisters to bring them up to speed. They're overjoyed to hear from me and have a ton of questions. We laugh and cry, and they get really upset when I describe my close call with Daniel and the chase in the ocean. They want to come down to support me on Friday, but I encourage them to wait until the actual trial in a few months. They agree but might take their turn coming to see me so that I can have support. It's a kind gesture, and I appreciate it.

Next, I put on some music, play with the kittens that I will have to say goodbye to soon, spoil Bozer, who is getting back to himself, and feed my fish. I hear a noise at the back door just as I'm about to start supper. Bozer is hobbling along ahead of me. I grab my bat, ready to defend myself if need be. I open the door ready to swing when I hear, "Whoa, Marina, put that bat down. It's me, Brian. Don't swing."

I let my breath out in a huff and ask him, "What do you think you're doing, sneaking in at the back door? Are you trying to give me a heart attack?"

"No, I'm sorry, but I wanted to bring in more firewood for you and check the back to see if it was secure."

I hold the door open for him to pass by me and realize it's been a while since he's checked in on me. "Glad to see you, Brian. Thanks for being neighborly and looking out for me."

"Where is everybody? I haven't seen Matteo in a long time. How is everything?"

"Well, they're at the lawyer's office and should be back soon. Matt is doing well, although he'd sure like to get his patent before the trial, so he's feeling the pressure."

"I bet. Well, Liam and I have been working hard to get things rolling with the Daniel case. I can't wait to see that man get what he deserves, so he can't harm you anymore."

"I appreciate your concern, but I've chosen to forgive him and not to worry about the outcome. Hey, would you like a kitten for the barn? Do you need another mouser in training?"

"I can't believe you're being so nonchalant about the whole thing. No, I don't have time for kittens right now, but thanks."

"Alrighty then. Would you like to stay for supper? I'm making my famous sesame salmon recipe and it is simply delicious!"

"Twist my rubber arm. How can I say no to that culinary feat?"

Right at that moment, Mindy and Matt return home with papers in hand, ready for the hearing scheduled for the next day. They seem surprised to see Brian since there was no other vehicle parked in the driveway, but quickly recover and start small talk with him, while I prep the fish. Mindy jumps in to help with stuffed mushrooms and a Greek salad while filling me in on her meeting. I tell her about my experience at the beach and she is amazed at the redemptive process.

We dive into the food, with light banter about our respective days, and everything tastes delicious. Brian is pressing for details on the case, but Matt is pretty tight-lipped and just barely answers his questions. I divert the topic with blueberry pie and French vanilla bean ice cream. Our taste buds dance to life and our conversation turns bright. The power of a sugar high is not to be minimized, and I take full advantage by bringing out Settlers of Catan and declaring that the winner gets out of doing dishes.

They set up the board while I serve tea, but I suddenly bend over in excruciating pain. Mindy excuses herself to go to the bathroom, and I have to leave the room to let some air out. The guys are looking a bit green themselves, and I begin to question whether my fish was off. All of a sudden, we're all running for the nearest toilet and can't get there fast enough. The stench is horrible, and as I run upstairs to my bathroom, I don't quite make it before getting the runs. Oh Lord, what did we eat? I hope the repercussions are just dirty clothing and don't require a hospital visit. The picture doesn't get any prettier, as now there is retching involved and it's coming out of both ends. My stomach is in turmoil. I get changed and head downstairs to check on the crew. The stench hits me like a ton of bricks, and I have to control myself not to vomit on the poor guys who look like they just lost their best friend.

"What the heck did you feed us, Marina? Are you trying to eliminate us? What is the deal here?" questions Brian.

I plug my nose while shaking my head and point to the offensive leftover mushrooms on the counter. "No, I swear, I received these nice mushrooms from a friend who must've picked the wrong kind without knowing it. I would never do that on purpose," I harrumph. "I will get you some ginger ale to soothe your stomach."

"No thanks, I am going home to change my pants and straight to bed. I will think twice before dining on your delicacies," mutters Brian.

I escort him to the door with my apologies and try not to take his words to heart, as I know it's just the pain talking.

Matt is holding his stomach and says, "I'll take that ginger ale offer and haul myself to bed to sleep this off before the trial. Don't worry Marina, we will find this quite funny in the future when we're all feeling better. It was no fault of yours. He's just venting, and now we have the blessing of an early night to get some rest."

I can hear Mindy calling my name from her bedroom, so I rush over and see she is looking pale and quite ill. I explain about the poisonous mushrooms and all she is worried about is, "I'm sorry I can't clean up, but I think I have to stay low for now. How is my Matty holding up?"

"Well, he is sick too but in good spirits, whereas Brian left in a sick huff, but Matt assures me this will be quite a funny tale when it's all said and done."

She grunts, squeezes my hand and closes her eyes. I gingerly tiptoe out to the kitchen, hoping she'll be alright. I must warn my friend about those mushrooms before she gives some to others. I send her a text and find Matt with his head on the table, eyes closed, hand out reaching for the cup I offer him. I give him a quick neck massage and he groans, so I help him to his room and slowly walk up the stairs to mine. So much for a fun evening beating them at Catan and getting out of dishes. I guess I will take care of that on the morrow.

CHAPTER FIFTEEN

I'm surprised that the text from my coworker states that she got the mushrooms as a gift from a guy but decided to pass them along as she detests mushrooms. Now that makes me wonder if this was a setup all along to get us sick or near death before the trial. I ask her to describe the man who gave her the bad mushrooms, and it sounds like one of the guys I saw at the cabin. But how would he know that she would pass them along to me? It could all be a fluke. I shouldn't jump to conclusions with no concrete evidence. I dismiss it from my mind, so I can focus on getting myself prepared for what lies ahead. I start off by reading from the book of Proverbs to receive some nuggets of wisdom and I pray for a clear and discerning mind.

I feel a lot better, both mentally and physically. I think a smoothie might be the best idea for my empty stomach this morning. Mindy emerges, grabs a glass of water, and heads back to rest as she confirms she's not quite up to snuff yet. Matt appears bleary-eyed but can hold a conversation, so that's a good sign. I offer him a smoothie, which he gladly accepts, and we discuss the proceedings and what to expect. His lawyers might tune in for the actual trial if needed, but we'll take it one step at a time. I had to cancel work for today, so we will all drive in together as moral support and take our turns on the witness stand. I am feeling a little nervous as I have never testified in court before, but this will be good practice before the real deal.

I choose a sophisticated black and white outfit with high heels and put my hair up in a chignon to look as professional as possible. Matt comes out in gray pants and a blazer and looks quite dapper. Mindy appears in a white pantsuit that sets off her red hair, and her complexion looks a lot better. We grab our notes and transcripts, and after feeding the pets, we head off in the truck, praying all the way.

We're ushered into a waiting room where the lawyer is waiting to instruct us. Matteo gets to testify first, then myself, followed by Mindy. We will be sworn in first, then need to stick to the script and answer the questions concisely. We're here to lay the foundation, present enough probable cause to show that Daniel committed the crime, and present our evidence.

We have time to focus, recenter our thoughts, and sip our tea while Matt is doing his best to show Daniel's intent. Before I know it, it's my turn. I give Mindy a quick hug as I'm escorted into the courtroom. It looks intimidating, but I walk as calmly as I can to my seat. I mistakenly glance at Daniel and see a sinister look in his eyes, as if he's mocking me. I have to remind myself not to react but to keep my focus centered on the truth. My flesh would love to send him a sassy look back, but I restrain myself and get ready to begin.

The whole ordeal goes by in a surreal way, as if I'm not part of it but looking down on the proceedings, somehow participating and answering the questions without faltering. I feel confident, and I speak clearly. It's as though I'm getting heavenly help with the words I hear coming out of my mouth. The cross-examination is intense, and they're trying to badger me, to get my feathers ruffled, and to get me to lose my cool, but none of their tactics affect me. The judge examines the photos taken at the beach with my cell phone that show Daniel bound in the back of the truck, the gun used, and the date on the back. My lawyer manages to get Daniel's real name as being Tim Fuller and rattles his testimony to shreds. I am officially done presenting and defending my testimony, so I am escorted out the back door as Mindy comes in the side door for her turn. I shoot her a smile and walk out into Matt's waiting embrace as we head outside to wait and get some fresh air. We share our courtroom experiences and find out that his testimony went smoothly as well, and it was good to finally know our attacker's real name. Matt figures the real Daniel Blackmann will be contacted and required to stand trial for his involvement in the case. He may need to involve his local scientist friend to verify his invention and intent.

Mindy emerges blinking in the bright sunshine and looking a little deflated. She informs us that she was rattled and might not have answered as well as she'd have liked. We encompass her in a sandwich hug and decide to go out for a celebratory meal, having survived the first round. We pick Pete's Diner, known for serving the best burgers in town with calamari and homemade roasted garlic aioli sauce. We're excited to hear all about Mindy's experience and debrief when I notice two burly guys trying to appear nonchalant but failing miserably, staring at us from a corner table. Great, we've been followed. I didn't see them when we came in. I motion with my head and we quickly change topics and steer our conversation to safer waters. Our own narrow escape memories on the water resurface, and all of us are trying to figure out how we're going to get out of this pickle this time. I wonder if we should get Liam involved as a backup in case these punks try to follow us home. I take out my phone and send him a text. I know he's probably still at the courthouse, and maybe Brian is still around to help out.

We decide not to panic or show fear but continue to enjoy our meal while waiting for Liam to indicate he's in place, ready to follow them. I think we should pay, then start to drive towards the beach, and Liam can head them off. I can't wait for all this to be behind us so I can enjoy a normal meal without looking over my shoulder. It's funny how you don't appreciate little things until those very freedoms are taken from you.

Ping. I hear Liam's text come in, double-check to make sure, then wait five more minutes by going to the washroom while Matt settles the bill. We walk out casually and slowly start to drive away, laughing at how the guys are trying to get their meals to go in a hurry but finally give up and come rushing out. Time to face the music. I am confident in Liam's ability to fend them off and know which road to take that will give him the best opportunity for the showdown. For this plan to work, we may have to play cat and mouse and pretend to get caught. Matt is trying to talk me out of it in case something goes wrong, but I really want these guys to finally get caught, and the only way is to catch them red-handed. I instruct Matt to send Liam a text about which road he can hide on while we set the trap.

All is going according to plan as I pull out to a lookout point over the ocean and get out to take pictures. Of course, true to style, they pull up behind us with guns pointed at us, but instead of waiting, one guy rushes me and bowls me over down the steep embankment. As I'm flipping end over end, I'm wondering what went wrong with my perfectly laid out plan. I hear the guy grunting as he's also somersaulting above me because he miscalculated and ended up following me downwards. I hope his gun gets pried out of his hand in the descent. I think I should enroll in a self-defense course. I might need a few tactics up my sleeve. Thankfully, my sister took a course and taught me how to kick a guy's knee to break it to slow him down, and then I can kick a little higher if all else fails. I am also asking God for protection and a way of escape once we reach the bottom. Good thing there are mostly ferns and moss but I am selfishly hoping he hits a few stumps and rocks to slow him down, but that might be false hope.

I stop and quickly check for any broken bones. I hop to my feet and let adrenaline take over as I keep running down the path to safety, veering as I go. A bullet whizzes by my left ear, so I veer right. It seems to always work in the movies. I feel led to make a sharp turn and see a huge rock wall with an opening where I can hide and catch my breath. Then, I see the guy running past and getting swiped from the side by Brian. The gun goes flying, as well as some choice words, while Brian manhandles him on his face with his arms behind his back in no time and cuffs him. I am impressed with his skill. I might take lessons from Brian instead!

The coast is clear, so I emerge from my hiding spot, and Brian motions for me to go ahead where I see the road that will lead me back up to my truck. Instead, I see Matt driving down wildly with Mindy hanging onto the dashboard, so I wave to show them I am unharmed. He barely puts it in park and flies out the door to deposit me into the truck safely between them, asking questions and thanking God at the same time. I want to hear what happened to the other guy and if Liam apprehended him before anyone got hurt, but we're all talking at once. I laugh and motion for them to drive a few more meters down to the beach where we can wait to meet up with our brave crew.

The view always takes my breath away and calms me. This is something I appreciate at the moment. Matt and Mindy are taking out the leaves and dirt from my hair while filling me in on guy number two. Liam did an expert takedown and is presently pumping the guy for details as to who hired him and so forth. Matt is mad that I got out of the truck first because he wanted to be the bait. "What were you thinking, putting yourself in harm's way like that?" He yells.

I shrug, "I acted on instinct, perhaps impulsively. Besides, it all worked out and we got the bad guys in the end."

Matt groans, pulls a curl, and says, "I want to be your knight in shining armor to show off my amazing abilities too, you know."

"Well, you gotta be quick when Marina is let loose." pipes in Mindy, smiling at me protectively.

I feel their love surround me like a warm embrace and breathe in this moment of togetherness, then breathe out the stress of my latest escape. I reach for each of their hands and thank God for protecting us and helping us conquer our would-be assailants once again. They add in their gratitude as we watch the glorious colors of the sunset fade to allow the moon its time to shine. I need to let my partners shine with their talents too.

The moment is broken with Brian and Liam tapping on the window, peeking in to see if we're all in one piece with no broken bones, and giving me a lecture on putting myself in harm's way again.

I nod, "I think I am learning to be more of a team player. Thanks so much for nabbing those guys for us. It could've turned nasty, but I see they're cuffed in the back seat of your ghost car. I assume they'll be escorted to the precinct for further questioning."

"Yes, we have photos, evidence, and the proof we needed to finally make our move on these hired crooks, thanks to you, Marina," Liam admits. "But please be careful and let us do our job."

I humbly nod again, thinking that the point has been made crystal clear and I will take it to heart. Brian asks if he can get a lift back to his house while Liam deals with this in an official capacity. We slowly make our way back, rehashing our harrowing day.

At night, I select my dad's extra-large khaki T-shirt that I keep as a reminder of him. I smell the fabric, but his scent is long gone. Whenever I want a hug from him or I'm feeling homesick, I wear his shirt as pajamas to bring me extra comfort. I also keep his white handkerchief with the blue border on my night table. I use it whenever I need a good cry, and remember all the times he'd whip one out of his pocket whenever I needed it. I sure miss those days. Dad's hankies were always his signature style and something I would buy him for Christmas. I guess I need a dad hug tonight, so I will receive one from my heavenly Father as I fall asleep, praying I don't have any nightmares from today's events.

CHAPTER SIXTEEN

I love waking up from a dream about my dad where I get to interact with him just as I remember him; whole, healthy, full of life, teasing me with that twinkle in his eyes and not one sign of cancer in his body. What a gift from God and one that I will treasure by writing it down in my journal to remember.

Thanksgiving weekend is upon us, and I, for one, have a lot to be thankful for this season. Our tradition is to cook a turkey, served with stuffing, mashed potatoes, gravy, cranberry sauce, a pickle tray, broccoli salad, and pumpkin pie for la pièce de résistance. But I am open to seeing what Matt and Mindy usually cook up, as I enjoy trying new foods and cultures. This reminds me of all the mission trips I've taken with my family, choirs, and ministry teams. Music has opened the door for me to sing in Ukraine, through the States and Canada, Holland, Denmark, and the Cayman Islands.

I could write a book on each of these trips, but here are some highlights. When I was fifteen years old, I had the opportunity to go to Ukraine for the first time with my parents and four friends. The iron curtain had just come down, so the people were all mobbing us for Bibles, and they all wanted to know about Jesus. They treated us like royalty, stood in breadlines at 5:00 a.m. just to feed us their very best, and culturally we were expected to graciously accept it, knowing they wouldn't eat for a week. It was very humbling indeed. There were beautiful memories, cultures, and people. That trip was life-changing for me, and I sure appreciated Canada a lot more when I returned; our freedoms, drinking water, free clean bathrooms, and food in abundance.

I joined a choir at Bible College and had the privilege of going back to Ukraine and experiencing the beauty of singing in cathedrals with amazing acoustics that sounded ethereal. Holland was so beautiful with its fields of tulips, windmills, and friendly people who wanted to experience the presence of Jesus.

Denmark was so pretty with its canals, history, and cobblestoned streets. We had the opportunity to repair a roof in Amsterdam in the drug section of town and show love to the people affected by addictions.

The Cayman Islands were so gorgeous with turtles, crystal blue waters, and contagious island music. We got to serve in a church, working on landscaping as well as doing skits, puppet shows in the schools, and singing on the rocks overlooking the crashing waves. A fish did bite three of my toes. I reacted by kicking, and thankfully, it released me with my toes intact and just a blood trail as proof. I might've jumped into the nearest guy's arms to protect myself as I thought I'd been attacked by a shark, but you would've had to have been there to see it. The moral of the story is not to wear red nail polish or you can become quick bait. It was pretty neat to snorkel for hours with barracudas, swordfish, sharks, and colorful fish in the beauty of the coral reef. Hundreds of stingrays would congregate as the tourists would feed them. I wondered why they smeared fish food on my neck until the stingrays began to suck it off of my skin. It was a scary, squealing ordeal! I have my own secret technique of attracting fish, as I accidentally got seasick from the wild catamaran ride and was instantly surrounded by exotic fish. But I digress from asking my guests what they usually serve for Thanksgiving dinner.

"Good morning, sleepy heads. I'm wondering if you have any special requests for Thanksgiving dinner," I ask as they head for the coffee pot.

They both shake their heads. "No, we don't usually celebrate that holiday in Venezuela, so we're open to experiencing your version," replies Matt groggily.

Mindy adds, "I look forward to helping you in the kitchen and adding a few spices that will remind us of our culture too."

"What a great idea!" I exclaim. "I love learning new ways to cook and trying new foods."

"I'm going to get three kittens ready to go to their adopted families tomorrow at church, and maybe you guys would like to tag along."

"Sure, it's about time I met more of your friends, and now that the two guys are hopefully out of the picture, I can move about more freely," comments Matt. "Let me now cook you up a fabulous breakfast while you two relax and chat by the fire."

We giggle and traipse to the living room, each grabbing a kitten to have some final snuggles and some girl talk.

Mindy starts by fishing to see if I have any interest in a special man at church like Brian or Liam, but I assure her that we're just good friends.

"Yes, but do they know that? They seem to have feelings for you. They might like a chance to see if your relationship could develop into something romantic. Of course, you'd have to pick one and the other would be out of sorts, but it's better than stringing them along."

"What?" I hesitantly add. "I have not encouraged or led them to believe there was anything more than just friendship, or so I thought.

But if I'm honest, I guess I've been enjoying their attention and thoughtful care instead of letting them down gently so they can move on. But they've never asked me out or made the first move, so we're all getting along fine and it's okay to continue in friendship."

"Let me see it from an outsider looking in," Mindy remarks. "It seems like they're mighty protective of you and wouldn't mind duking it out over you if they had to, but would like to genuinely know if they even have a chance."

"You're too funny, that just happens in the movies, but I will take your candid observations to heart," I reply.

Matt appears in the doorway and announces that breakfast is served. We don't need to be told twice as this is quite a treat. We put the playful kitties back in the box to see French toast, sausage, and fruit salad all specially laid out on the table.

"Matt, you've outdone yourself this time," I wink and nod appreciatively.

We all dig into the gourmet brunch while I delicately ask how the final stages of the invention are coming along. "When will I get to be in the know?"

Matteo sighs. "It's been quite the fight and process, but my dad is actually helping out big time in these final preparations and I can't wait to share all the details with you. It's not safe yet but it will be very soon."

I reply, "It still sounds mysterious and if it's like 'soon' in the Bible, I could still be waiting a long time but I know it will be worth it in the end."

They chuckle and smoothly change the topic to going for a hike along the coast to get some great pictures and exercise. I agree with their plan as hiking is a favorite pastime of mine and I have some great views and trails to take them on. Bozer usually comes along, but his leg is not up for jumping boulders and logs quite yet. I will put the turkey in the oven before we head out, and we will come back to our aromatic feast.

I change into my hiking pants, merino wool shirt, boots, and a waterproof jacket to be prepared for all weather and elevation changes. My backpack has trail mix, jerky, first aid kit, rope, knife, bear spray, tarp, water, extra socks, and matches. I like to be prepared as this trail is pretty steep and has some picturesque waterfalls, a suspension bridge, and tricky terrain to maneuver. I let Mindy borrow another pair of hikers and a jacket, and off we go to explore the beautiful forest and coastline.

We park at the trailhead, grab our day packs, and head off single file up the mossy trail that will bring us to our first lookout. I lead the way as I know which forks to take, using my hiking poles to help me climb steep ledges and cross the creeks. We feed the whiskey jacks trail mix from our hands and we stop at the first lake for some pictures. In the summer, I'd be jumping in, but the frigid waters keep me out at this time of the year. There are still some very ripe blueberries to pick and mushrooms to identify. The next loop leads us to the suspension bridge overlooking a tall waterfall, with the mist creating rainbow colors. It is breathtaking and provides more pictures for us to stop and take.

My favorite part is the lookout coming up with the ocean view that fills the horizon. There's a bench that was built out of a huge log so we sit and have our picnic lunch. Croissant egg sandwiches, pickles, brie cheese, and apple-lime juice complement the experience. Everything tastes better outside, far from any amenities. We begin to list all the things we're thankful for; like Matt's newfound faith, the gift of forgiveness, that our lives became entwined through adversity, blossoming friendships, creativity, and hope for the future.

I sense we're being watched and the hair on the back of my neck stands at attention. I look behind me and don't see anything besides trees. Matt senses my apprehension and grabs his knife from his pocket while turning to scan the bushes. Mindy screams, and I see a cougar perched in a tree ready to pounce.

I instruct them to stand tall, maintain eye contact, and begin to walk back down the trail. I have my bear spray aimed in one hand and a hiking pole brandished as a spear in the other. We will have to leave our lunch behind in hopes it will get distracted and lose interest in us. His yellow eyes follow us, tail whipping side to side, and I feel like I've become the prey. My heart is racing. My instincts tell me to run, scream and get as far away as possible. But then, I decide to use prayer as a weapon.

"I command you, cougar, to submit to the spirit of God within us. I take dominion over you and command you to be docile. You will not attack in Jesus' name."

I have always wanted to try that and my faith is pretty high, so I am expecting full cooperation. Mindy starts to pray out loud too, and Matt is just concentrating on positioning himself in front of us to protect us. So far, so good. We've managed to get twenty feet away, and the cougar has leaped down to finish off our lunch. I hope it is enough to satisfy his appetite. We continue to walk backward at a faster clip until the trail takes us out of sight and we turn and hightail it out of there. We breathe a sigh of relief. I'd rather see a bear than a cougar any day. I remind the others to keep a sharp eye out as it could still stalk us down the mountain. We don't linger or enjoy the views as much as we'd like because of our close encounter and will feel safer once we've reached sea level and are closer to my truck.

"I don't know about you guys, but you've sure spiced up my life since I've met you," I say. "I don't think I've ever had this much adventure in two weeks in my life! I'm trying to figure out if you attract danger or if this is normal life for you."

"Well, it does seem a little more action-packed lately, but only because of the nature of my invention and its near completion. Normally, I can invent without too much interference, but you will understand why when all is fully revealed," states Matt.

"I await with bated breath, let me tell you," I reply.

Mindy chuckles and agrees that it has been more intense than usual. It should abate once it is all licensed and made public.

We make it down the mountain with no more cougar sightings, but who knows? It's possible it silently stalked us and we were never the wiser. We enjoy a private cove and explore the shore for new shells, sea glass, and colorful crabs. The wind starts to pick up, so we head to the truck to escape the chilly sea breeze. We thank God for His protection once again and look forward to our feast awaiting us at home.

We all work together, prepping the stuffing and cranberry sauce, mashing the potatoes, stirring the gravy, and setting the table with my special orange tablecloth and matching cloth napkins. I light my pumpkin spice candle and serve the cranberry and ginger ale punch in wine glasses while Matt carves the turkey. Voila, now it is time to feast, banter, and celebrate His faithfulness.

I challenge them to a game of Rummy-O so I can redeem my title. Lo and behold, I do win, so Matt will have to honor our previous agreement and take me out for dinner on the town. He blames the turkey for making him lethargic, but I remind him that I do love numbers too. The next part of our evening involves pumpkin pie served with whip cream, coffee, and a last snuggle with the kittens by the fire. A good relaxing evening was very much needed, topped off by a soak in the hot tub to take away the aches from the hike and twinkling stars to bid us good night.

I can tell that Matt is preoccupied tonight. I can only imagine that he will feel like a burden has been lifted off his shoulders once this is all completed. But I find out the true source of his thoughts when he pulls me aside before retiring for the evening.

"Ah Marina, I've been thinking and praying and I wanted to ask you a personal question. You can answer now or sleep on it if you like," he begins hesitantly.

I sit back down with him by the fire and turn to face him. I can see the vulnerable look in his eyes.

"We've been through a lot together these past two weeks. I realize we haven't known each other for very long, but I wanted to express that I'm developing strong feelings for you." He takes a deep breath and continues. "I understand the timing is not the best with the trial looming and unresolved business, but I would really like to know if I even have a chance with you. Would you be interested in seeing where this relationship might take us? I've noticed you have a few close guy friends here, but I am hoping to be your one and only if you are open to that idea."

I think about Brian, Liam, and Rocky but how I never felt released to explore where those friendships might take me. Then I think about Matt and feel different somehow. I trust my inner knowing as I have been praying about this and feel ready to give him an answer. My silence is killing him as he looks about ready to burst from waiting so I quickly get him out of his misery.

"Sorry for the delay, but I like to process my feelings." He nods and keeps his eyes on me expectantly. "I feel like our friendship seems different to me on a romantic level, so I am open to seeing where this road might take us." I smile into his eyes and see them misting over with joy.

He pulls me towards him in a tight embrace, and I squeeze back, excited at what God has in store for us.

I do have those butterfly feelings whenever he's around. I can't wait to be with him after that, but this all feels so new. Is it only because of the intense adventures we've shared? I'd really like to see how we are together when life is humdrum, normal, and boring. My heart is telling me one thing, and my mind is trying to keep me grounded. However, I am ready to take the risk of opening my heart to love. Now I can introduce him to my friends at church and see their reactions. He releases me, jarring me from my contemplations, and I already miss his nearness. Oh Lord, I'm sounding like a sappy girl already. I need to journal my thoughts and hope to sleep tonight. He takes my hand and leads me to the staircase, where we part ways for the night, each to our own musings.

CHAPTER SEVENTEEN

I dreamt of being chased by a cougar, of budding cherry blossoms and new love, of picnics by the sea, and I remembered why as I wake up. We had the talk last night; I didn't imagine it. I feel like I'm soaring on cloud nine. I want to shout it out to the whole world and will have the opportunity when I introduce him at church. Then I recall that I should have the talk with Brian and Liam beforehand, but maybe I can avoid it and they can join the dots themselves. No, I should not dodge confrontation just because it'll make me feel uncomfortable because I would want to know if I was in their shoes. Perhaps a letter expressing how much I appreciate their friendship, but it feels awkward to throw Matt in there, so face-to-face is the better option.

My Bible reading for the day in Proverbs is centered on friendship and choosing the right path. James 4:17 (MSG) nails it home with, "If you know the right thing to do and don't do it, that, for you, is evil."

OK, I will obey. I receive the message loud and clear. I hope for the right opportunity to do so.

I start making blueberry pancakes as I hum a new song when I feel masculine arms wrap around me from behind.

"Oh, good morning to you. How was your sleep?" I ask, turning to reciprocate the hug.

His resonating bass tickles my ear as he responds, "The best I've had in a while. My dreams were filled with a cute auburn chick who kept challenging me to new conquests."

"Hmm, sounds like an intriguing woman," I murmur. He's about to zero in for our first kiss when I hear someone clear their throat, so we quickly part.

My face feels rather heated. Matt has a scowl on his face for being interrupted, and Mindy is smiling at me knowingly.

"I see there have been new developments. My role as chaperone has just gone up another level. Marina, you and I have some catching up to do. I can't wait to hear all about your side of the story," quirks Mindy.

"What about my side of the story, huh?" Matt asks.

She playfully shoves him to the side to get some coffee and says, "I know all about your side of the story, Matt. I've been watching you fall for her these past two weeks."

I serve breakfast, and then I fill her in on my thought process since we last chatted. I value Mindy's input and wisdom. She cautions me to take it one step at a time, deal with my two guy friends up front, and let the dust settle before rushing head over heels into something new. She advises that Matt should stay at Brian's or a hotel if this budding romance is going to continue. These are great points to ponder and discuss.

Matt enters the room with an official-looking manila envelope that was delivered to my door. We all hold our breath, anticipating the news inside. It contains the judge's verdict in fancy lawyer talk that basically states that we have a case and the trial is set for December 14, two months from now. We were hoping Tim would plead guilty but that's not the case. A lot of legwork is ahead of us, but we are up for the challenge.

I notice it's time to get ready for church. I pack the kittens in a box and prepare myself to be honest with my two guy friends. Matt has promised me a dinner date for beating him at Rummy-O, and I am only too happy to oblige.

The church is packed, and the music and message are moving as I see people respond to God's love and adoration. We're surrounded by my friends who all want to be introduced to Matt and teasingly affirm that he is real and not imaginary after all. I see Liam motioning me over, so I excuse myself and see that he wants to confirm that I received the news about the trial.

"Yes, we did, and thank you again for all your hard work that has gotten us this far. I also wanted to mention to you that I appreciate your friendship and skills. You always want to keep me safe..."

He interrupts me with, "I've noticed you and Matt getting close, and I want you to know that I am happy for you. I won't deny that I wish I was in his shoes, but I will continue to look out for you if that's OK."

I admire his candor and vulnerability. "You are too kind, Liam," I respond. "I've always looked up to you. I accept your offer with gratitude."

We part amicably. I must admit, he let me off the hook very easily and gentlemanly.

Three children run up to me asking if they can see their kittens, and I cannot deny their enthusiasm, so I ask them to follow me to my truck where their gift awaits. I love seeing their joy as they're reunited with their purring bundles. I can remember my excitement as a child when I received my first kitten. I feel a pang as I say my goodbyes to my fluff balls but I'm assuaged by the fact that I can visit them anytime.

I notice Brian is hanging back in the parking lot waiting to chat. I divert my attention to him and notice his body language looks dejected with his head down and hands in his pockets. He must've also noticed my chumminess with Matt, and I feel for him.

He starts with, "I see you're parting with your kittens. Maybe I should take one to comfort me, as I also see you're choosing to part with me, correct?"

"Oh Brian, I've always wondered about us but there was no action taken to ask me out, so I figured you might not feel the spark," I counter.

"Well, I wasn't sure how you felt and did not want to take a chance to ruin our friendship. But in retrospect, I see that I should've been bold and taken the risk so as not to lose out in every way. Did I ever have a chance with you, Marina? Please be honest so I can learn from this and move on."

I search his eyes and see hurt that I wish I could erase. He has asked me an impossible question that will pierce him sharply no matter how I answer.

"A girl always wants to feel like she is worth the risk like her man had the guts to fight for her. You are an amazing guy, and now you just have to believe in yourself and take a chance on love. I don't think you truly loved me. You liked me and the idea of us but deep down I know you would've found the courage to ask because you are brave. I know God will bring the woman that will set your heart on fire, I was just a spark."

I feel like my prayers were answered and the Holy Spirit gave me the words needed to bring completion and a release I didn't know was lacking to move forward. Mindy was so right, and I'm glad I heeded her advice to handle this head-on and not just sweep it under the carpet. Those friendships meant something to me, and now that those doors are closed, I am free to open my heart to a man that came into my life like it was scripted in heaven. I believe God likes to write our love story if we will only let Him and not get in the way of His perfectly laid out plans.

I also think that I can continue my friendship with Brian and Liam, but in a brotherly way with no strings attached or flirting. It's as if once you've found the one, a person should close the attraction door and put a "not available" sign on their heart so that it is guarded and kept for that special someone. I think every mother should explain this concept to their daughters to avoid a lot of unnecessary heartache and disillusionment. The enemy loves divorce and likes to use this tool as a weapon to always want to search for greener grass, but sometimes, the person just needs to tend to their yard, pull the weeds, and not covet when things get tough, or so my mother taught me.

The desire to be at the beach to experience the calming effect of the ocean is overwhelming, but I must rescue Matteo from the gaggle of girls who are clamoring over him. I chuckle at his expression of bewilderment over all this attention, and I too am swept away by questions from my friends all at once. I raise my hand to shush them and exclaim that I will fill them in at our next soul sister's night, which gets us off the hook for the time being. We grab Mindy and head out the side door to escape the crowds as we gun it home to enjoy Thanksgiving leftovers, namely shepherd's pie with gravy, turkey, mashed potatoes, and veggies. So, yummy even the second time around. I was taught to not waste food, so leftovers are a huge staple in my house.

An afternoon nap is required to complete our day of rest, but I'm sure Matt is getting more work done on his project. I would love to be a bug on the wall to get a sneak peek, but I won't push the envelope. All will be revealed at the appropriate time. Patience is one trait I could practice and get better at as waiting is hard for me. But I've learned from experience that when you rush things or get ahead of God, you tend to struggle; but if you wait, things turn out smoothly, without a hitch. I could jeopardize the whole thing, and I do not want to risk it because of my curiosity.

Instead, I write a letter to Matt, explaining what I'm going through so he understands the struggle since I'm choosing to honor and trust his judgment. I will give it to him tonight at the restaurant, which gets me in motion to change into the special burnt orange dress that makes me feel like a princess. I add my expensive perfume, brown high heels, and a cream shawl in case we walk by the ocean in the twilight. My motto is: 'a girl always has to be prepared,' so I throw in some hiking boots just in case.

I quickly call my sisters and mom to let them know I'm going on a first date with Matt. I haven't had a chance to share the news that we are an item with them yet. They would be upset to learn about this important development after the fact. Of course, it is fun to involve my family and get the squeals and bursts of excitement that this type of news generates. I am not one bit disappointed by their reactions. They cannot wait to meet him in person. They would like to see pictures and assure me they will be praying for us every step of the way. That was fun. Now, onto the real deal. I should go see if Matt is ready yet.

Mindy exclaims her approval of my fancy outfit. She hugs me, tells me I look beautiful, and motions me to the front door, where Matt is waiting to escort me to my car. He is looking suave in his navy-blue blazer and beige pants, and he smells divine. A true gentleman, he bends to open the door for me.

"You look amazing in that color." Matt leans in to place a light kiss on my cheek. "I love how it makes your hair seem like it's on fire."

"You look quite dapper yourself. I am looking forward to some quality time together. Where are you taking me tonight?"

"Well, that is a surprise and you will just have to wait and see, my fiery girl."

He starts to drive in the opposite direction of town and instead heads towards the mountains. Now he has me intrigued.

I settle in for the ride and begin to share about my conversations with Liam and Brian so that he knows that I've closed those doors and been upfront with my two guy friends.

"I noticed you were deep in conversation with Liam but assumed it was about the case," he says. "I am so glad you broached the subject with him and am honored that you've chosen to give me a chance. I'm not surprised at Brian's reaction. I could tell he really liked you, so I will give him some space and be mindful of him. Thank you for having the courage to handle this with maturity and grace. My respect for you has gone up even more."

He reaches over and caresses my hand while keeping one hand on the steering wheel. I gaze at the beauty of the majestic peaks topped with snow, with the sparkling blue-green ocean to my right, and thank God for this place I call home and this man He's brought into my life.

I wonder how Matt knows these roads and where he is taking me.

I glance at him sideways, and he smiles knowingly and remarks, "I do have my own connections. Besides, I was here for a few months before I appeared on your doorstep."

"Right, we haven't discussed much about you before your appearance in my world, which would be very interesting. Care to enlighten me," I ask?

"I promise you I will divulge a few personal details tonight, but you must wait until we get to our destination, my fair lady," he quips.

God is working on my patience again, and I didn't even ask for more. I know from experience that it is a scary prayer that always seems to get answered.

"How about questions about your dating life before me?" I venture.

"Ah. Now that is a journey I can take you on." He exhales and continues, "I've only dated three girls before you and I learned a lot about what to do and not do. Of course, having two sisters also helped in that department, as they were always hounding me to share my feelings and communicate openly, which some guys find hard to do. My first girlfriend was very controlling, so I listened to advice from my closest guy friend, who had just escaped his own nightmare of a manipulative relationship, and he told me to get out before I lost my own identity. I saw the truth in his words because I was confused and getting more disillusioned daily. It was a hard decision because she was my first love, and I thought I could fix her brokenness, but I quickly realized that I could not be her savior."

I hold his hand and comfort him.

He smiles and continues, "The second girl was short-lived and I regret letting her take me down the path of no return," he says. "I should've been strong enough to resist her but I did not listen to that still small voice and that is one gift I can never get back. If only people would realize that one moment of passion can lead to a lot of devastation that has ripple effects and affects many more than just themselves. One selfish act wreaks havoc on family members, the church community, and later on that special woman who really matters."

I squeeze his hand as I can see the tears in his eyes at the realization of what this will cost his future wife. I am amazed that he dared to share this so early in our friendship and that he wants to be above board on every level. I appreciate that but I'm also saddened at the consequences of sin. I know he's forgiven, but these matters always bring baggage. Is this something I can live with, sacrifice, and accept? I will have to compartmentalize that information for now and journal about it later on.

"Thank you for sharing those intimate details," I say softly. "It shows me you are not perfect but that you are honest and won't hide the nitty-gritty. I know you've been forgiven, so I cannot hold that against you as God remembers it no more. I am not naive enough to think that there are no repercussions, but I trust that once those soul ties are broken, healing can take place at a soul level."

He nods and takes a deep breath before moving on to the third one. I think we're sharing too much information too soon in our relationship. My heart does not want to hear any more details right now. But I think we've been through such intense situations together that we've forged an unnaturally strong bond early on, so I might as well hear him out. Then I can decide if I want to commit or not. I think I will have to bring this to God in prayer and even a time of fasting to see if this is the man for me. I take a deep breath myself and let him know I am ready to resume listening.

"The last girl was a rebound fling that I had no business even entertaining, but I swallowed the enemy's lies that I had gone this far already and there was no use in abstaining anymore. I was hardened by sin and went with the flow of the world instead of repenting, turning away, and making it right with God. It did not last long, and eventually, my conscience caught up with my actions. I decided I could not live this way any longer, so I ended it and walked away. I was ashamed of who I'd become but I knew I'd made the right decision to try to walk on a different path from that point onwards. It's been four years. I haven't dated since. I've been laser-focused on this project."

"Whew, that is a lot to take in. Do you realize that the enemy likes to heap shame on you, whereas the Holy Spirit convicts, sets you free from shame, and gives you the grace to move on? There's a saying, 'you can't change the past, but you can write the present.' I've seen God redeem what the enemy meant for harm to become someone's greatest victory."

"Yes, I'm beginning to see how that is possible, and it amazes me that God can use our brokenness to help others avoid the same pitfalls." He smiles. "How about you? Did you lose your heart to a lucky guy?"

"I've had close guy friends but never felt released to take it to the next level of dating, so I refused all offers, and here I am. Of course, I experienced infatuations, emotionally got involved, and dreamt of more, but I never did anything about it. I've never even been kissed and I'm saving that for a special guy."

"Wow, that blows me away," he says. "It shows me the difference when God is at the center and how special it is to wait for His perfect plan. You made the right choices, and what a gift you have to offer to the right man, which is how God designed it from the beginning," replies Matt in wonder.

The view opens up to a beautiful lake with a cabin nestled along its shore. I am surprised that I never knew this existed and I marvel at how private and perfect this place is. The door opens, revealing an older gentleman waving, smiling, and motioning us over to join him on the scenic deck.

"Welcome my friends, I trust your journey was picturesque. Come, make yourself at home by enjoying this view," he gestures.

Matteo introduces me to his scientist friend, Hulio, who is brilliant and has been indispensable with his research and connections.

"Ah, your fame precedes you, as I have heard of your incredible contributions. Pleased to meet you," I exclaim.

He opens his arms wide for a hug and kisses me on each cheek, making me feel like family already.

"Your beauty has preceded you and I have heard of your rescue operation as well," remarks my new friend, sending an obvious wink to Matt, who is grinning like a schoolboy. "No worries, Matteo, I have prepared everything to your specifications, so relax and I will begin your special evening with chilled drinks and hors d'oeuvres of braised prawns with garlic bread."

I am led to a settee and a beautifully laid out table with wild tiger lilies, matching cloth napkins, and silverware sparkling in the sunlight, and I am impressed with the attention to detail.

"It's as if someone knew my favorite flowers, color, and taste to a tee," I wonder aloud. "How can this be?"

"Mindy might've had a part to play" replies Matt. "Please come and drink in the beauty of this place. It is your turn to receive and be served."

This is exactly the sanctuary my soul needs after our conversation, and I relish the privacy of not having to deal with a crowded place. How thoughtful of Matt to go to all lengths for me. The water reflects the mountains and clouds, and I see fish rising to catch their supper. There are lily pads, and I wish I had a fishing line to throw in the still waters.

"This date is not going exactly the way I planned it," Matt says. "I didn't think I would be sharing my past so soon. I understand this may have upset you, and I don't wish to presume I still have as good of a chance with you but know that I will give you the space and time you need. I was hoping to dazzle you but I'm kind of glad this came up so you know right from the start and you can make an informed decision about me."

"There are things I will have to come to grips with, but let's just enjoy what you have planned and our scenic surroundings," I reply.

He nods gratefully and starts snapping photos of me and the lake while entertaining me with stories of his youth. I regale him with my own, and soon we're laughing at our childhood antics. The prawns, garlic bread, and sparkling apple juice are delicious, and I can hardly wait for the main course. Much to my surprise, leek soup and lobster with a side of garlic mashed potatoes ensue.

"How do you get lobster out here?" I ask my grinning escort, who is looking quite pleased with himself at the moment.

"I have my wily ways," he cheekily responds.

Sometimes I just want to pinch his upper cheek when he is acting so smug. I restrain myself and also my desire to kiss him, as that should be his first move in my books.

The sun is beginning to set at this altitude, and I am bedazzled by the twinkling white lights that line the cabin and lead to the gazebo by the lake. It's a romantic setting. I might just get my wish, after all. We shall see how the evening progresses.

Hulio is an excellent host, knowing when to appear, when to give us privacy to talk, and when to insert jokes to lighten the mood. He finds us nestled close together to ward off the chill, so he brings out cozy blankets and a tiramisu dessert with espresso coffee to top the evening off. Then, jazz music fills the air from outside speakers. I'm amazed that Matt thought of everything, or is it Hulio's touch?

Things get a little mysterious when he takes me by the hand and brings me to a cleverly hidden doorway that leads underground to a chamber lit by torches. My heart starts to beat faster when I realize he's about to disclose part of his invention. This means he must trust me enough to take this important step. As my eyes adjust to the lighting, I see three clear tanks filled with a liquid that could encompass a human body while lying down. Interestingly, there are bubbles like an ionization effect is occurring and a silicone mask fitting that would presumably be placed on one's mouth and nose to allow for breathing while immersed. I turn to Matt with raised eyebrows, waiting for an explanation. He looks pretty excited to disclose it.

"This is my baby, very dear to my heart and so close to being realized," he says slowly with a huge smile. "These tanks hold half of the secret to curing cancer of any kind. The other half is with my father, and that would include a trip to see for yourself. The reason why I needed to be at this location is that the minerals found in this lake and the deposits in the soil combined with the salt water of the ocean create a cleansing effect on the body while purifying the organs affected."

I am overcome with emotion as I know I am witnessing a cure and a miracle right before my eyes. I turn to hug him and squeal with delight. I laugh, twirl, dance, and stomp my feet for victory over this deadly disease. At long last, no more pain, fear, anxiety, or slow tortured deaths for so many people that the enemy loved to inflict.

It's no surprise that people were trying to steal, kill, and go to great lengths to copy or destroy this unique creation. I am curious as to the other part that completes the process, but I'm overwhelmed at the magnitude of this incredible solution that will change the world.

"Matt, this is so amazing," I exclaim with a huge grin. "I cannot fathom how you came to figure this combination out. I can't wait to hear all the steps involved, the journey that led you to this point, and how you will proceed to tell the world. I am awestruck by the wonder of it all. You must've been guided by God's hand to figure out the complexities and enlightened to bring them all together. I feel like I would want to shout this hope from the rooftops. I can't even imagine your excitement. How did you test this solution to find out if the desired result was successful?"

Hulio clears his throat behind me, saying, "That, my dear, has been the most rewarding part to witness of anything I've experienced in my lifetime," he says. "Our organization carefully selects the candidates with a rigorous screening process of utmost security and confidentiality and works closely with one main doctor, who happens to be a cancer specialist. He knows the history of each patient, performs the before and after tests, and is intricately involved every step of the way. Dr. Burado is undone by seeing the majority of his patients recover with no trace of cancer. Their cells are healthy and the DNA damage is reversed. It truly is a phenomenon to behold and life-changing for the individual. I suspect the hand of God was involved in guiding Matteo to the exact solution needed to destroy any prions, annihilate all cancer cells, and restore the electrical and magnetic frequencies to perfect harmony and balance. A true miracle indeed!"

Matteo has tears in his eyes as he begins to recount the many lives transformed by this new technology. He now realizes God's handiwork and gives Him glory for revealing the steps and bringing the right specialists and the team to make it a reality.

"I know it's too late for my mother and your father, but I picture them looking down from heaven with total joy that no other precious human being has to suffer. A cure has finally come to fruition and will be released to every person, rich or poor. That is the fight that we're in right now, to keep greedy pharma out of the equation so they can no longer abuse, withhold, or control the masses all in the name of money, the only god they serve."

I feel the need to sit down to absorb all that I've just seen and heard. It seems like this is a selah moment that is found in the Psalms to pause and reflect on what has just been said. It feels like we're on holy ground and I sense the presence of angels guarding, protecting, and aiding this whole operation to keep it secret until the appointed time of unveiling.

Hulio brings me a cup of cold water. As I begin to ponder the big picture, many questions start to arise, like, what are the differences in composition between the three tanks; how long does it take before a person is cured; what happens when the minerals run out; have you found a way to replicate the soil components; and is there another location in the world that has this same unique formula? However, the moment is too sacred to waste on satisfying my curiosity, so I will focus my attention on these two dear men who have reason to celebrate.

"You two make a great team, and I feel honored that you would choose to trust and share this with me on such a unique first date," I say. "I understand the challenges ahead. I will support and help you fight the opposition to release the cure that will impact countless lives. The magnitude of this breakthrough is mind-blowing and we need all of heaven's armies and a team of intercessors to succeed against the powers of this world that would try to jeopardize this cure from ever seeing the light of day."

Matt can tell I'm feeling overwhelmed, so he takes me by the hand and leads me back up to the lit pathway that guides us to the lake. I take a big breath of fresh air and begin to realize the stress and pressure that he must be under.

"How do you do it?" I ask. "How do you handle the strain that comes with this on so many fronts?"

He gazes deep into my eyes to allow me a glimpse into his soul.

"I choose daily to only focus on what I can do and rely on my team around the world to each do their part. So together as we pool our resources, passions, and gifts, the vision is manifested and brought to life. It's incredible to be part of such brilliant talent and see what can be achieved when we all unite toward one common goal."

We haven't missed the glorious pink-hued sunset, which would usually have me scrambling for my camera, but tonight is a night to be in the moment, to relish, relax, rest, and enjoy His creation before me. I marvel at all the experiences that have brought me to this moment. I feel like I've been living a different life these past two weeks, like in a fast-paced movie.

Matt moves behind me and pulls me back into his arms as we take in the setting fireball. I feel a flame building between us and I want to let my guard down and let him in. He senses the shift as I melt into his embrace. He slowly turns me to face him and seems to be asking for my permission, as he knows this is a big step for me. I yield, and he gently moves in to seal the evening with my first fireworks kiss. I savor the moment as I feel the glow reach the end of my toes. The twinkly lights combined with the glittering stars and the moon beginning to reflect its path on the surface of the calm, miracle-giving lake, make for an incredibly romantic atmosphere.

CHAPTER EIGHTEEN

L ast night felt like a dream. I awake with an urge to journal about the myriad of disclosures and emotions. Today is Thanksgiving Monday, and I can rest in bed at my leisure as I don't have to rush to work. I begin by listing all the things I'm thankful for, then processing my feelings about Matt's past, which takes two pages of heart-wrenching pain. I continue journaling with the discovery of the sought-after invention, which fills three pages of awe, questions, and process, concluding with the experience of my first kiss. My apprehension of not knowing how to kiss vanished as it felt very natural, right, and special. He made me feel as though I was his first and most prized gift. The ride back was filled with sharing our hopes, dreams, and wonder at how God orchestrated our paths to cross in His perfect timing.

I even shared with him the story of how I was born two and a half months premature. I weighed three pounds and thirteen and a half ounces, making me a miracle baby. I was placed in the incubator for three weeks as my life hung in the balance. My body was filled with tubes and needles all over, even my forehead, as my veins were too small in my arms. My loved ones would delicately reach in and rub my belly with two fingers every time the monitor beeped, signifying I needed to take a breath, as preemies would forget to breathe. I stayed one more week free of the incubator and increased in weight to five pounds and five ounces before going home. I still have a bald spot in my bangs and a dent in my forehead that shows where the needles were inserted. I actually fit nestled in my dad's big hand and wore doll clothes.

My mom's heart stopped for one minute after I was born as she was hemorrhaging after the C-section. She actually died as her spirit whooshed out of her mouth on an exhaled breath, then rose to the ceiling where she was looking down at a person on the operating table. Suddenly, she saw a nurse slapping the woman's face to revive her and drifted down to see that it was her body. She wanted to come back to kick her butt, so her spirit came back in through her mouth and her heart started beating once again. I'm so glad she had the fight and not the flight instinct as I cannot imagine my life without the best mom in the whole wide world.

Matt then kissed my dent and bald spot, telling me how glad he was that I fought for life and how that strength still permeates who I am today. We talked about our desire to meet each other's families and his dream of flying me to his headquarters to meet his father and see the other half of the cure. Maybe even meet some of his healed patients who can describe the whole process. I am intrigued and would love that opportunity.

Unbeknownst to me, Matt is already planning the details for his private plane to pick us up and whisk us away for a few days. I walk out to the sitting room where I see the handwritten note explaining the details and asking if I will be able to take some time off for an adventure trip. Mindy comes in humming happily as she exclaims that she is invited to join us, and she cannot wait to see her brother in the flesh. I am excited to go, so I quickly make a few calls to get a soul sister to house-sit and inform my students that I will be away. The joys of being self-employed include a flexible schedule.

"I was going to ask about your date, but I can tell from your rosy glow that it went well," Mindy says. "What do you think about the discovery?"

"I am overwhelmed at all that I saw and all that was divulged. I think it's absolutely incredible! I understand so much more now, the importance of his work and the attack against it. I can't wait to see part two to take in the completed work. I am excited to meet his father and a little nervous at the same time. Our relationship is still new, and this is all happening so fast, but I am enjoying the wild ride!"

There's a knock on the door, and Brian is nervously standing there. He asks if he can pick up a kitten if I still have one to give away. I motion him inside and lead the way to the box where he can choose from the two that are left. He picks up the gray male with a white patch around its eye, and the kitten begins to purr as it climbs to his neck, resembling a scarf.

I laugh, "It looks like a match made in heaven. You're made for each other," then I realize that might not have been the best choice of words.

He winces and asks how the case is progressing. I shrug as I haven't heard much except the date of the trial. I can't wait until it is all behind us. He thanks me for the kitten, and I sense the loss of our friendship and how my one decision has affected our twenty-year friendship. His eyes still look pained, and I feel bad for my part in it, but I believe that he too will find the right mate that will complete him.

Lastly, I call Liam to keep him in the loop about our absence for a few days. I ask him to keep us posted on any new developments. He cautions us to be alert as he is feeling uneasy with how cocky Tim's behavior is even behind bars. I assure him we will do everything in our power. I thank him again for going above and beyond on our behalf.

A thrill goes through me as I race to my bedroom to pack a few classy outfits, toiletries, and some lounging clothes for the evenings. I can hardly wait to experience Matt's world as he's encountered mine. I will learn a lot more about him when I see him interact with his colleagues, dad, and friends. He wants to keep the destination top secret so that I won't know exactly where his hidden lab is, to keep his confidentiality intact until the cure is revealed to the masses. I'm fine with that. I understand that it is a privilege just to be brought into his inner circle and I can play dumb for real if I'm questioned.

Matt appears at my door with the biggest grin on his face. "What do you think of my crazy last-minute idea?" He asks. "I can hardly wait to show you everything and especially show you off to my father and friends. This feels like Christmas morning to me!"

I laugh as he twirls me around my bedroom, and I assure him that I'm just as excited. He grabs my suitcase, takes my hand, and pulls me along to hurry to the truck where Mindy is already waiting. Talk about wasting no time. Once Matt decides on a course of action, the plan is put into motion with no delay. It's a good characteristic to have. He is a doer and follows through on his intentions with confidence. I'm learning more about him already and we haven't even left the tarmac yet. Hang on for an epic ride.

He whisks us away to the airport, and instead of going into the terminal, he drives to the hangar on the far side of the airfield, parks in his reserved spot, and introduces me to his crew. The pilot is checking his list but takes the time to greet us. The stewardess ushers us aboard a sleek-looking plane, while a businessman in a suit hands us confidentiality papers to sign and takes a seat opposite Matt. Mindy and I sit adjacent, and I marvel at how efficient everyone is at their role. This is like a smooth operation with many moving parts, knowing exactly what their function is and doing it masterfully.

As the men discuss business, Mindy smiles at me as she's been here before but is looking at this through my eyes as a first-timer and says, "You ain't seen nothing yet, my dear. Relax and enjoy the scenery. Take a few deep breaths because your senses may be on overload for the next few days."

Matt casually looks over, reaches for my hand, and gives me a reassuring squeeze as we prepare for takeoff. The flight takes two hours and I assume we're in the States as we land at a private runway where we're greeted by a chauffeur in a black Mercedes. The royal treatment is making me feel like a princess, and I can't help but grin like a schoolgirl. Matt is scheduling our itinerary while making calls to make sure everything is ready for our arrival. The drive takes twenty minutes, and we arrive at a pristine white warehouse with a welcoming lobby filled with sunshine streaming in from the huge front windows. The classy space lends itself to a feeling of excellence, and I am impressed already.

The receptionist rises to greet Matt with a welcome hug and leads us straight through the back offices to the main warehouse, which is buzzing with activity. Everyone stops when they notice Matteo has entered the room, and they all begin to clap, shout, and stamp their feet in response to the incredibly great news that preceded our arrival.

A tall, distinguished man officially announces, in a loud, proud voice, "The long-awaited, five years in the making, the final formula has been tested, approved, patented, and is ready to be launched! Matteo has figured out the last component and all systems go are in effect! We have obtained a green light to begin full operational systems. We are proceeding with full steam ahead and are officially the first team to have reached the end goal of a cancer cure to be released worldwide! Our hard work, research, invested time, and countless hours have made our dream come true. Thank you to every team member who has committed their lives to this cause. We couldn't have gotten to this point of culmination without you. I honor my talented son who defied all odds and never quit. Even though others thought he was crazy, he persevered to find the solution and conquered this terrible disease with God's help and science. Bravo!"

I look with astonishment at Matt, who humbly acknowledges his team, points up to give glory to the One who helped him every step of the way and beams with joy at his family. What a moment to celebrate. I had no idea he was this close. How come he never shared this with me last night?

As if reading my thoughts, he approaches and whispers in my ear, "I was dying to tell you but only got confirmation at 2:00 a.m., so I have been busy preparing ever since and wanted to surprise you. Surprise, my sweet ocean girl, we did it! We beat the bad guys in the end, and they can no longer torment, threaten or destroy us. I have the patent in hand, approval from the government, health authorities, and higher-ups, so this is a major victory!"

I zero in on a kiss that will knock his socks off, which is my way of surprising him, and I succeed beautifully.

I am interrupted by someone clearing their throat, and I blush to my hairline when I see his father regarding me with a curious air. Matt quickly recovers and hastily introduces me as his girl with a confident smile, and I am surprised once again when Theodore embraces me in a big bear hug.

"I'm so happy to finally make your acquaintance, my dear. I have much to thank you for coming to my son's rescue after the stabbing and taking care of him ever since. I must say I was curious to meet the woman that stole my son's heart within a week and had the bravery to stick with him through thick and thin. I heard all about the dangers you've encountered even without knowing what you were fighting to protect. Well done, Marina. You are as much a part of the team as any of us here."

I like him already. "Pleasure to meet you, sir. I'd like to in turn thank you for raising such a fine son who has risen to the challenge and succeeded where many have failed in not only a cure but in obtaining my affection," I respond with a wink.

Theodore laughs and comments that I will fit right in with that kind of spunk as he winks at his sister, who nods her agreement entirely.

"Come, come, let me show off our beauties that you haven't had the privilege of seeing. This is the counterpart that completes the cure and is magnificent to behold. I call them..." He is interrupted by Matt, who takes charge by blindfolding me.

"Now father, this is my baby and I want to be the one unveiling the other half if you please. You cannot steal my thunder."

Oh, I sense some rivalry, good-natured competition, and a desire to outdo the other, occurring between father and son. Interesting, but do I really need to be caught in between their oustmanship (I like to make up new words that fit the sentiment) and be blindfolded?

"Is this really necessary?" I ask plaintively.

I am guided by holding onto each of their arms, one step at a time. When I am released from the blindfold, I blink rapidly as my eyes try to adjust to the light.

"Voila, you are witnessing the other half of completion. Allow me to introduce you to the capsules of light that will forever change how we do and view science," explains Matteo triumphantly.

What I see before me are upright light capsules that have room for a person to stand, while other capsules are horizontal to allow the patient to lie down restfully while receiving their light treatments.

"You see, the light heals all organs, cells, tissues, or skin affected by cancer by penetrating at a cellular level and reversing the effects of the disease. The first half you saw at the lake is to rid the body of all toxins and inflammation, ionize the cells, and get the body ready to fully absorb part two. One has to be washed clean to receive full healing at every level. Tank 1 has the soil deposits; Tank 2 has the mineral concentration; Tank 3 holds the ionized salty brine for complete hydration. Each step builds on the other and takes twenty minutes per tank. When the body is encapsulated in a light capsule for forty-five minutes here, the effect is a complete restoration of the DNA and destruction of all diseased cells," concludes Matteo.

Theodore cannot help but add, "Our team then proceeds under the guidance of Dr. Burado to fully scan the body to be 100 percent certain that every trace of cancer has disappeared, and only healthy cells, DNA, organs, and tissue remain. We have witnessed this miracle in 500 patients thus far, who have totally been cured with no recurrence and have returned to living healthy, grateful lives."

"I am at a loss for words at what I'm witnessing before me. This is truly staggering and I'm overjoyed at the hope this will give to millions of people and the families affected. Thank you again for persevering through all the obstacles to help all mankind. We are forever in your debt," I manage to choke out.

"That is another thing," Mindy exclaims. "We're hoping to offer this at a reasonable price with the help of government backing that can utilize the funds effectively now that a cure has been fully realized. Therefore, low-income families will have access to the cure just like the rich and powerful. This is the last piece of the puzzle that is being put into place in legal terms to protect the cure from those who would hope to control it for their personal gain. That dilemma has been my passion and area of expertise that I've been working on behind the scenes with an amazing legal team at my disposal, hence the red notebook."

I nod as I remember wanting to peek inside that little red book and refraining myself due to our friendship. So many things are coming to light, and I'm amazed at all the gifts, talents, and passions needed to make this dream come true. Marvelous indeed!

"Well, let's celebrate at a fancy restaurant at 6:00 p.m. tonight. The chauffeur will bring you to my place to freshen up and rest after your flight," replies Theodore.

That sounds like music to my ears. I even packed a chic black dress for the occasion. Matteo takes my hand and leads the way, greeting his colleagues personally. I sense the mutual respect and camaraderie between his team. Amazing things can happen when everyone is working on their gifts, collaborating, and striving for the same goal in love and unity, much like God's desire for His church.

Our car ride is filled with excited chatter about the implications of having the patent and the busy days ahead. Matt is so filled with gratitude that all is going according to plan and the visit was timed perfectly to announce the big victory. I am taking in all the new sights and notice that we're entering a busy city.

Theodore's house is like a modern version of a penthouse, with a view of the city, river, and mountains. There is even a top balcony where you can lounge on the roof terrace under the stars with potted palms and flowers beckoning. We're greeted by a maid who shows us to our rooms, and mine has a kitten sleeping in the sunlight, which makes me feel right at home. The room is tastefully decorated in hues of blue, and I take a power nap to infuse myself with energy for the evening celebrations.

I am awakened by a knock on the door, revealing Mindy, who looks resplendent in a purple gown that reaches to her elegant matching heels. I whistle and ask her to stay while I model my dress to get her opinion.

"Well, it is pretty but more suitable for tomorrow's luncheon.

However, I noticed a royal blue gown was left by your door that looks to be about your size. How about you try that one on to compare," Mindy replies with a knowing smile.

She brings in a beautiful box with a fancy blue dress folded neatly inside. I squeal with delight at the sight of the exquisite gown fit for a queen.

"I wonder who thought of this detail at the last minute," I muse.

The dress fits like it was made exactly for my petite frame, and I marvel at the silky material with an embroidered bodice and matching shawl.

"Oh, it fits you beautifully," Mindy exclaims. "You will be the belle of the ball."

She helps pull my hair into an updo and touches up my makeup, fluttering around me with special care. It makes me wonder what is going on tonight.

Matt sees me coming toward him and smiles appreciatively, "I see you've made my selection come to life with your beauty. Come, our chariot awaits."

Sure enough, there is a horse-drawn carriage with white horses waiting for us on the street.

"My sweet Matt, you have outdone yourself. Thank you for the dress and this surprise. You sure know how to make a girl feel special," I gush excitedly.

"Mindy will meet us there shortly. We have time to relax for the thirty-minute ride, and I can show you the sights along the way," replies Matt as he helps me into the carriage.

He steals a quick kiss that takes the chill away quite nicely, and I snuggle in, ready to explore this new city through his eyes. We visit art museums, science centers, fancy restaurants, and statues to entertain us until we arrive at an upscale restaurant, where we are ushered to a private dining area.

All at once, I am surrounded by ladies fawning over my dress and trying to gain Matt's attention. He apologizes in my ear, glides over to his father's table, and introduces me to the guests as his significant other, which casts an icy air over the ladies section and I smile sweetly in return. I find out that these guests have all contributed to the cause, either monetarily or as support, and have gathered to hear the big announcement. I scan the room of about fifty people and notice a table with guests who seem especially thrilled to be here. Matt sees my gaze and explains that they're the grateful patients who have been cured of cancer and have been part of the pilot program. Amazingly, I would love to chat with them and hear their stories.

The evening progresses with delicious entrees, followed by braised lamb, rice pilaf, and grilled avocado, all cooked to perfection. Before dessert is served, Theodore delivers a congratulatory speech to his son and announces that we are patented, approved, and ready to launch in all major countries. The deafening roar of applause is provoking silent tears to stream down my cheeks at the impact of this global reach, delivering hope to millions of people. I am surrounded by scientists, doctors, and investors, all congratulating Matteo, slapping him on the back, and shaking his hand in utter amazement that the long-awaited day has finally come! I am witnessing the most brilliant scientific breakthrough in my lifetime, and I'm overcome by the staggering impact this will have on the world.

I am beginning to also realize the implications for my own private life if I am to stay by Matteo's side. It will be like living under a microscope as a public figure. Am I ready for that kind of spotlight on our lives? I will have to share him with the world through global news, magazines, TV shows, and interviews. I am such a private person. I'm not sure I am ready to live under such scrutiny. Matt will be so busy with the launch that I'm not sure our two-and-a-half-week relationship can survive such a shift. I pull myself out of my selfish reverie. I will focus on this celebratory moment instead of worrying about tomorrow. I feel like a turtle emerging out of her shell. I remind myself that there are personal sacrifices involved with such a discovery, but I can process the pros and cons later.

I find myself gravitating to the table where the healed people sat, wanting to experience their joy at having a second chance at life. Before me is a vibrant twenty-year-old, Grace, who is sharing how she was at death's door with stage four colon cancer. She was selected as a test candidate and was given a clean bill of health by her doctor. All the cancer cells have been eradicated and her colon was renewed by the light therapy. She is going to finish her degree in medicine and wants to dedicate her life to being a part of this team. Wow, how intriguing to see her healed and now wanting to participate in seeing others cured.

Everyone wants to share their survival story, and I am swept away by their exuberance. It would be so neat to document each person's journey.

Lydia approaches me with her face shining with a radiant glow, telling me that her pancreas was cured of every trace of cancer. She is now looking forward to the future with her grandchildren and being there for her youngest child's wedding next month.

Maybe I've found my part to play and can't wait to share with Matt this new idea germinating within me. Speaking of which, he appears at my side to whisk me away to the dance floor where jazz music is being crooned as couples sway to the exquisite melodies. It feels as though no one else exists in the room as we zero in on each other and get swept away by our deepening love. I feel a tap on my shoulder as Theodore claims the next dance, and Matt graciously obliges his father.

"So, my dear, how are you doing under all the new pressure and attention that this kind of exposure brings?" asks my doting partner.

"Well, to be honest, I was feeling overwhelmed when I focused purely on myself," I reply, "but when I heard the testimonials of those getting a second chance at life, I was able to change my perspective and focus outwardly instead on the betterment of all mankind."

He nods, commenting that he's never seen his son with this kind of love glow before and he's very happy for him, but he knows this cure will forever change his way of life.

"I'd like to extend my help, guidance, and protection to you both for anything you need. I know the public eye can be taxing on one's need for privacy and normalcy," he comments.

I thank him for his kind regard and notice how his fatherly influence and trustworthiness makes me feel safe already.

"Anytime you feel the need to retire, just signal the chauffeur and he can take you ladies home to rest as there will be more festivities tomorrow," Theodore replies.

Again, he is looking out for our needs, and I appreciate his kindness. And then, Matteo claims me back to his side to greet a few more of his friends, sample some crème brûlée, and do one more twirl on the dance floor before I signal that my feet are killing me and it's time to make my exit. He helps Mindy and me to the car and promises to meet me at home before too long.

Mindy and I chat about the people we've met, the lives that were impacted, and my Cinderella evening on the ride home. The evening culminates with a hot sudsy bath, comfy PJs, and retiring to the rooftop to take in the city lights and twinkling stars.

I sense Matt's presence as he tries to sneak up behind me. I sigh in contentment that he was able to come and join me to enjoy this moment.

"How did you manage to pull yourself away from all your admiring fans?" I ask demurely.

He laughs, "Well, I knew who was waiting for me and politely made my excuses to be here with you, my love."

"Very wise man, making good choices for us already," I tease, "That merits you a kiss under the stars."

He does not disappoint, and I enjoy the moment of shared love, precious time together with just the two of us, and this incredible night.

"Marina, thank you for visiting my world. Seeing you here confirms my feelings that you belong by my side. I wouldn't want anyone else to share this special night with but you. Even with a room full of people, I knew where you were and always wanted to be near you. You've entered my dreams, you've stolen my heart, and I love you just the way you are. You mean the world to me, and if you prefer a quiet life, I will give all this up for you and pass it on to my very capable team.

"I can remain anonymous and work quietly in the shadows, as I don't desire the limelight of fame. I choose to give God the glory for this incredible breakthrough. I was missing the last link, but He directed me to the formula after meeting you. I know you value your quiet country life and I've come to love it too. Let's pray about this together over the next few weeks and see what God has in store for us as a couple."

"I think you've concluded well to bring it to God in prayer. I could go either direction right now, in terms of following you into the spotlight or keeping to the quiet life. I did have an idea that I wanted to share with you after hearing all the results from the cured patients at the party last night. Could I start by chronicling their testimonials in a reader-friendly format that the world could read about and be encouraged as to the effectiveness of your discovery?" I ask.

"That is a splendid idea!" Matt exclaims. "I could easily see you blossoming with your writing talent, and bringing hope to the world," remarks Matt excitedly.

We continue to share our hopes and dreams for the future and reluctantly force ourselves to retire for the evening.

CHAPTER NINETEEN

I wake up to a purring kitty on my chest and take her in my arms to see the sunrise coming up in brilliant shades of pink. Today's luncheon is all about honoring the team that has put in many long hours to bring this project to fruition, and I'm excited to meet everyone. My black dress is perfect for the occasion, and I feel like a million bucks as I skip down the stairs to see what's for breakfast. I run into Theodore, who is ready to rock in a gray power suit. He pulls me into a gentle morning hug, asking how my evening was with his son, with a twinkle in his eye.

"You raised a very talented, loving son who is quickly becoming my best friend and confidant. It has been really neat to see him in these surroundings and observe a different side of him that seems to shine and flourish. I know he is probably already thinking about his next invention as his mind is always creative. God has gifted him, and I can't wait to see what's next on the horizon."

"Yes, I can see he's quite taken with you. You seem to bring out the best in him. Your nature complements and strengthens him, so he has the space to create and you see him for who he really is, not just what you can get from him. I appreciate your relationship with God, and I notice that Matteo is honoring God with this project and seems stronger in his faith. That is important to me too. It may not be public knowledge as I am a very private person in my faith, but I look forward to sharing that side of me with you both."

I am overjoyed at hearing this from his heart and flash him a dazzling smile, taking his extended arm to go enjoy a light breakfast together.

The scene that Matt witnesses upon entering the kitchen is that of his father and sweetheart reading the Bible together, and he is taken aback at his father's openness.

"Well, you two look cozy. Mind if I join?" asks Matt.

Theodore pats the spot next to him and explains, "We were just discussing the finer points of healing and how God still heals today. Wouldn't it be neat to document miracles even before they go through our cure? Marina was just sharing her passion to write about the patients' stories, and an added part would be to pray for people first and see them healed. I love the idea. We could have a healing room with twenty-four-hour prayer and worship right beside us as an alternative first step for those who are open to that level of faith. It could also work for those waiting to get in, as I'm sure there will be long waiting lists and I think many miracles could occur right there!"

Matt marvels at the transformation of his father, but maybe he just never saw that side of him or he is more open now. Mindy joins in with a resounding yes, and I can see that this new idea could very well be a family passion.

Matt was hoping to steal me for a few moments, but he needs to tie up a few loose ends before the luncheon, and Mindy and I are busy making shopping plans before joining them at the luncheon. I do manage a quick kiss and that will have to suffice for now. In a way, he looks like he's looking forward to going back to British Columbia so that we can have more time to ourselves.

The luncheon is very special as every person is honored. I love to see the faces of the team light up as they are rewarded with a bonus check and applauded for their achievements. Matteo gives a resounding speech about the rollout that is about to occur where new facilities are being built in twenty major countries around the world with the capacity to offer the two-step cure and containers containing the capsules are being shipped as we speak. Doctors, technicians, and support teams are being sent to train and ensure all proper protocol is being implemented in each location, with the follow-up being documented every step of the way. The responding applause is deafening and enthusiasm is contagious as I look around the room at their beaming faces. The energy in the room is palpable, and I am so proud of Matt and this team for the role they play in impacting people's lives.

I see that I too could be a part of this team and travel with Matt to different locations around the world or stay home with all the comfort and familiarity that I know and love. It is not a decision to be rushed into and one that I will take to God in much prayer, asking for wisdom and journaling to see where He wants me to be. I believe He works with our gifts, desires, and passions that He's placed inside of us. Our destinies are written about in scrolls in heaven, and I desire to accomplish all that God has ordained for me. He chose me before the foundations of the world were even created (Ephesians 1:4). I do not want to miss out on one iota of it. This requires me to involve Him in every decision and only do what He asks, which involves daily relationship and intimacy. Hearing God's voice is one area that I am passionate about pursuing and implementing in this new journey. Is Matteo the marriage partner that God has written about in my love story?

Matt appears at my side and whispers that he has another surprise for me planned for this evening. It will involve a casual supper at home and, hopefully, plans to fly back tomorrow evening if all goes well at the office this afternoon.

My curiosity is piqued, and I squeeze his hand, saying, "Your speech was wonderful. You're a very charismatic speaker, and I love seeing all these qualities as I see you shine in your element. I keep learning new things about you, my mysterious geneticist."

He gives me a sexy smile, promising many more facets to learn about him that will keep me on my toes. I like the sound of that as it speaks of exploring life together with more adventures to come.

As I am being driven back to the house to enjoy a relaxing afternoon, I am thinking of my family and wishing they could be here to experience all this with me. Mindy had to go to the office to work. I am free to journal and take the time to process all my reflections thus far.

Matt makes me feel alive, treats me like a queen, sees me for who I am, and respects my ideas. I don't feel controlled by his position because he is giving me the freedom to be me and loving me just the way I am. He's not trying to change me to fit his mold, which I appreciate. I respect his strong leadership skills. I love watching his budding relationship with God. I can see that he honors his father and treats his employees very well. The list of pros is filling up my page and the only cons I can think of are having to share him with the world, no privacy, and having to balance work versus play, but he is willing to give up fame for us. As long as he can create, invent, and continue to use his talents to be who God has called him to be, I believe he can be content and fulfilled.

I think I will leave that decision up to him, so there can never be a chance for resentment or the blame game to creep into our relationship.

I am looking forward to his surprise and I can't imagine what else he has cooked up for me. What an intriguing man the Lord has brought into my life, and He knew how much fun I would have in getting to know him.

I wear the new blue pantsuit that I found shopping with Mindy that has the softest material I have ever owned. I grab a ginger beer to settle my stomach, a book about Venezuela I saw on the coffee table, and climb to the rooftop terrace to enjoy some vitamin D while basking in the sun. I am oblivious to Matteo, who is happily cooking up a storm in the kitchen while preparing his surprise for me. I am awakened by my suitor, who is looking mighty pleased with himself with his confident smile and gleam in his eyes.

"I see you've been brushing up on my country's history and this fast-paced life has caught up with you," he teases, tucking my hair behind my ear.

I embarrassingly wipe the drool from my cheek and sit up, letting him take me by the hand to dinner downstairs, which smells divine.

The table is set for eight, and to my delight, I am engulfed by his sisters and the rest of his family. His single sister Lucia reaches me first with a big hug, then Sofia, who is holding her daughter, Ana, embraces me followed by Andres, her husband, who is grinning and can't help but exclaim, "We're so pleased to meet the woman who has finally captured Matteo's heart. Come let us enjoy this feast he has prepared for the occasion."

The feast consists of shrimp jambalaya with spicy chorizo sausage, rice, veggies, and an amazing sauce that has us vying for seconds while enjoying each other's stories of childhood escapades. I am so touched that Matt flew his family here to meet me, and they're already stealing my heart with their love and acceptance. Little Ana climbs into my lap as I feed her some peach cobbler and snuggles in while sucking her thumb, content to listen to our laughter. Matt sends me a loving smile. Sofia is sharing about her nursing career coming to a standstill after Ana was born and how she would love to work with Matt's program in her city. Andres is a carpenter, happily building houses, while Lucia loves her dentistry work and is dating a pastor whom she met while working on his teeth. We all laugh and want details of her new relationship, which seems quite serious already. Theodore is beaming to have all his family together and reaches for Ana, who I grudgingly give up to wash the dishes with the girls while the boys enjoy their manly talk. Sofia wants to hear all about our courtship, and I recount our first date while she applauds her brother for his romanticism. Mindy and Lucia are catching up while drying dishes, and I can't help but feel as if I'm part of the family.

I extend an invitation for them to come to visit me in British Columbia before too long. They're overjoyed at the invite as they would love to see their little brother's paradise that he has carved out for himself and can't stop talking about. We visit late into the night, sharing our life's adventures and trying not to wake up Ana, who fell asleep in Grandpa's arms with our carefree banter. Sofia is the first to retire with her family, and I pause in the doorway to thank Matt for his thoughtfulness in bringing his family out to meet me and spend some quality time together. We linger in our embrace, and I'm beginning to feel I've found where I belong. No matter where we are, as long as we have each other, I am home.

CHAPTER TWENTY

I am awakened by Matt's two sisters jumping on me. They wrap themselves in cozy blankets and sit on my bed, wanting more girl talk. I laugh at their antics as this is exactly what my sisters would do. Rolling over, I see that it is 8:00 a.m., so I can't be annoyed as they allowed me to sleep in. Our laughter is bound to awaken the whole house, and soon we're joined by Mindy, who is also treating us with croissants, coffee, and fruit. It's not even my birthday and I am treated to breakfast in bed. I like this family a lot.

The men have already gone to work, with Andres tagging along to see the production for himself, and we have the day to enjoy each other's company before we fly back that evening. Mindy has decided to stay for a week to help her brother before flying back to South Africa to check on things on the home front. I will miss her dearly but realize I cannot keep her indefinitely.

Matt will stay with Hulio at the cabin as he has to coordinate the soil samples and saline solutions to exact specifications for distribution. I will be on my own once again, hopefully back to my normal, boring life teaching with nobody trying to eliminate me.

The sisters are shocked at how many times our lives were in danger and we had to escape, only to be hunted by new thugs. But they are proud of their little brother who has managed to create the invention of a lifetime that means so much to anyone who has lost a loved one to cancer. Their mom would be proud to know that this disease won't endanger or be a threat anymore and that the cure will end the painful suffering for so many.

Our time goes by quickly, and before I know it, Matt is whisking me away to the airport amid a flurry of tearful goodbyes and hopes to see each other soon. What a whirlwind few days. I'm so glad I got to see Matt in his world, meet his family, and see his dream come true. We spend the plane ride back sharing our hearts and simply enjoying being together undisturbed once more.

"You know, my father and sisters adore you. You passed the family test too, by the way."

Oh, and I thought he was the only one on trial, but, of course, he would be noticing my interactions with his family as well.

"Oh, is that so? Well, I'm glad I passed, so does that mean we are entering stage two of seriousness, or should we wait to see if you pass my family's test?" I tease back.

"You do make a good point. I am more than ready to make that a reality," he concedes. "I could fly your mom and sisters over this week to see if I qualify as good husband material," he suggests.

I squeal with delight and throw myself at him to plant an invigorating kiss to seal the deal.

"I take it you liked that idea. Call your family to set up a time and we will make it happen."

As soon as we get home, we're greeted by Bozer, who is so excited to see us. I run in to hug and thank my friend for house-sitting while she promises to catch up at our next soul sister meeting and pet my cats. Matt is busy packing his few things to continue his work at Hulio's, and

I call my family to set up a time for them to fly down. We pick Friday, and I am thrilled that I'll see them after two nights of sleep. It's been a few months since we've all been together, and I'm already planning the menu, making my grocery list, and getting the rooms ready.

Amid the bustle, my phone rings, and I hear Liam's excited voice, "The trial has been dropped. You don't have to testify anymore! Tim pleaded guilty to murdering Sarena and stabbing Matteo! The two thugs were hired by Daniel Blackmann to take you out and he has backed down now that the patent and cure have been released. He lost his chance at stealing the formula and went berserk upon hearing the release and admitted to everything when questioned. The lawyers have been working around the clock to bring closure, and the judge will soon pass sentences on all those implicated.

"You are no longer in harm's way and can live a carefree life without having to look over your shoulder. I am still in shock over how smart Matteo is and how he managed to figure out a cure is beyond me. Please congratulate him for me. Welcome back home, Marina."

I thank him for the good news and call out to Matt, who comes running, thinking I'm in danger. I relay the fantastic news and collapse in his arms, feeling so relieved that this is all over and I don't have to go to court or worry about our safety any longer. He strokes my back and admits he had heard the outcome from his own lawyer but was waiting on the final word.

"I'm so glad you're safe. I'm glad that Tim has pleaded guilty, and Daniel will be prosecuted for trying to steal my work and bring harm to us. I choose daily to forgive them and hope they can, in turn, forgive themselves for allowing greed, ambition, and hatred to cloud their better judgment."

I smile at how quickly my man is learning to react in a godly way and not want retribution or revenge as the world might dictate. I am blessed indeed.

I don't want to see Matt go, but I understand he has to be on site for this next phase, and we will still have dates and make time for each other amidst the busyness. This will be a good test to see if our relationship can handle us being apart, prioritizing, and not neglecting each other. I will be distracted by teaching, my family coming and seeing how I can implement my ideas to write down every patient's success story of beating cancer. Mindy is my coordinator at the other end to help me set up my website so the world can follow along.

Matt is waiting for me at the door for a goodbye kiss and promises me that we will celebrate our win of not having to go to court tomorrow evening. I propose my idea of planning this date myself, and all he has to do is meet me here at 5:00 p.m. He looks pleased with my suggestion and can't wait to see what I've got cooking. I hug him for a long time and mischievously tell him to get back to work so we can play later.

I sadly watch from the window as he drives away, but I distract myself by calling my cousin Bo to see if I can introduce them to my beau and plan a date at their house. Rebecca is over the moon to finally meet this mystery man of mine and would love to put a roast in the oven with potatoes and carrots if I would like to bring dessert. Perfect, I will put together my famous blueberry cheesecake and reward myself with a soak in the hot tub, followed by reading my favorite book.

As I'm humming away baking, there's a knock at my door and Brian is standing there with a box of chocolates to congratulate us on our victory in the trial being dropped. I welcome him in for some coffee and he is astounded by the news of Matteo's cancer cure and can't believe that was what we were protecting and fighting for. Word is getting around and soon the newspaper will want a cover story as well as throw a big town party to celebrate. I'm hoping we can keep this hush-hush from the world about our special lake. Otherwise, this town will become a destination place to visit and will never be the same again. I know Matt is planning to keep his formula secret and just have designated cities with the proper equipment to treat patients to minimize exploitation. Brian knows me well enough not to press for details and is content to just visit and make sure all is well in my world. I assure him that I'm thriving and cannot wait to see my family, which makes him happy for me. I thank him for the chocolates, and he takes his leave, mentioning that his kitten is a godsend and is helping him heal, which makes me happy in turn.

The next day, I'm thrilled to see my students once again and notice how everyone is treating me as a celebrity, which I hope will fade with time. I grin and bear it as I know they mean well, but it proves to me that I treasure my private, simple way of life and I think Matt does too. I think this is another topic we can discuss at dinner tonight, and I'm looking forward to seeing the dynamics and interactions.

Matt arrives promptly on time, which I appreciate about him, and he whistles at my getup of cowboy boots and a denim dress. He gives me a twirl and I hand him a cowboy hat to match mine, and off we go in my truck, excitedly talking about our day. He was very productive and able to accomplish his goals, knowing I would be his reward tonight.

"I'm tickled pink that you would use me as a motivator, and I must admit you're a pretty good influencer yourself. I'm excited to show you off this evening."

"I'm guessing you're taking me to an old-fashioned barn dance to see my country moves," teases Matt.

"Just you wait and see, you might even be on trial tonight," I tease right back.

"Oh, I thought I passed the test long ago," remarks my hot date.

"Not quite, you've still got a week of testing, my love. I like to keep you on your toes, being the best version of yourself always," I smile back.

"That's exactly what I love about you, honey. You bring out the very best in me and expect nothing less, which makes me reach for the stars. I believe that I can be who God created me to be; fully alive in Him and able to do all He has set for me to accomplish."

I squeeze his hand while he sings along to "I Can Only Imagine" on the radio. I'm happy to note he has a beautiful voice, which just gave him five stars in my book. Another test passed with flying colors.

"Hey, do you happen to play any instruments?" I ask innocently.

"Of course, I play a mean guitar and can serenade you anytime you wish, my darling."

"Good to know, and yes, I might even ask you tonight, so be ready," I challenge with a twinkle in my eye.

"In case you haven't noticed, I was born ready. I will accept any challenge you throw my way to win your hand, my fiery Marina!" I respond with a bright smile.

We exclaim at the beauty of the ocean view on the scenic drive and can't help but pull over to take a few pictures and steal a kiss or two or three. I'm noticing we might arrive a little late, but it was well worth the delay. Matt whistles appreciatively as we pull up to the house and sends me a look that speaks volumes as he figures out the test for tonight, meeting the family!

The twins come barreling out of the house at top speed for hugs all around, with the rest of the family right behind them, chuckling at their joie de vivre. They welcome Matteo warmly and laugh at our cowboy outfits. They exclaim over how they finally get to meet the first man I've ever brought over, so he must be someone very special indeed.

They take us on a tour of the ranch, and I note how Matt seems to love horses and, by the sounds of it, is a good rider himself, which just bought him extra brownie points. Not that I'm obsessively counting or anything. Wink, wink.

Rebecca leads us back to the house to feast on roast beef, and Matteo decides to open up and share his big discovery, which leaves them all speechless. They turn to look at me in shock. Rebecca can't help but exclaim, "How in the world did you manage to keep this huge invention to yourself, Marina?"

I laugh, saying, "Now you know I can keep a top-level secret and can be trusted with juicy information. I just found out myself this past week and didn't know when I saw you last."

That comment got me off the hook, and Matt is having fun answering their myriad of questions all at once.

Rebecca pulls me aside to the kitchen to tell me her opinion of my man. "You picked a winner. He's handsome, intelligent, and attentive to you. I'm just worried that his attentiveness might wear off once he gets rolling with this cure."

I assure her we've been discussing this very thing and he's willing to remain hidden for the sake of our privacy. I also mention my mom and sisters are coming to visit, and she runs to inform the others, who squeal with delight at the prospect of seeing family.

My dessert is a hit, and we spend the evening playing games, drinking hot cocoa, and promising to see each other very soon. On the ride home, Matt expresses his delight at my date idea and the pleasure of meeting my family, where he felt at home and welcomed. I assure him he passed the test. I ask him if we should go horseback riding next time, and he readily agrees. We're looking forward to seeing the rest of my family after one night of sleep, and he is working out the details with his pilot to ensure everything is on schedule.

I start to share my feelings. "I appreciate your attentiveness to my family. I know your mind must be in 100 different directions at the moment. One quality I've noticed is how you can multitask, compartmentalize, and get things done without looking stressed or frazzled. How do you manage the pressure?"

"Well, my sweetie, I've been juggling this type of workload since my teens and learned early on the importance of surrounding yourself with a competent, trained team and delegating so all the burden does not all fall on my shoulders. You taught me to ask for grace daily. I know I can only do my part and not worry about the rest. Most importantly, I know how to prioritize. You are a huge priority in my life. I treasure you and will always make time for you. I've noted that quality time is your main love language."

"I'm amazed you already deduced what makes me feel loved. In case you're wondering, I also like physical touch, words of affirmation, acts of service, and gifts." I tease back, "I think your priority would be words, service, touch, time, and gifts. Am I right?"

"Pretty darn close, but I like them all as well. Just you wait and see."

If our goodbye fireworks at the end of the night are any indication, I think touch is right up there at the moment.

CHAPTER TWENTY-ONE

Today is the day! I fly out of bed ready to hit my to-do list, starting with polishing my bathrooms until they sparkle, throwing together my famous cilantro chicken lime in the crock pot, grabbing my grocery list, and heading off to teach.

"Variety is the spice of life" is one motto I live by, which makes me thrive.

My students pick up on my energy and apply themselves splendidly. Linda hugs me and is ecstatic about the launch. She wants to hear all the details, but I tell her I have to run to meet my family at the airport.

"We will catch up soon, my friend. I have so much to tell you," I hurriedly reply and run out the door.

I am so excited. I can hardly contain my anticipation of seeing my family all together again. Matt will come to eat with us tonight. I get my family to myself for a few hours of much-needed girl talk, wisdom, and advice.

As I park by the private hangar, I collect my thoughts and give thanks to God for all the steps that have led me to this incredible day. I get to introduce my family to the first man I've said yes to courting. It's a special day indeed.

I spot my sisters coming off the plane with scarves flying and suitcases following in their wake. Mom is busy chatting with the stewardess and most likely sharing her life's story of the miracles she's seen God perform, which opens the door to prayer and learning more about Jesus.

I wave, shout, and run to meet them, throwing my arms around them, thrilled to be reunited at last. It feels like Christmas came early. I squeeze my mom extra tight as it seems like I don't get to see her as often as I'd like. We're all chatting at once, but then they stop in unison to look behind me, hoping to meet my mystery man, and I shake my head, indicating with my hand that they will meet him at 5:00 p.m.

"You'll just have to wait to meet my man as I want you all to myself. We have so much to catch up on," I explain.

Mom takes me by the hand, examines me from head to toe, and exclaims, "You must be in love. You've lost weight, which means you're too lovesick to eat. Oh, I can't wait to meet him!"

I usher them to my waiting truck, put their luggage in the back, and we all hop in for a ride to the beach to take in the beauty of the ocean. I still don't take the sea for granted and so enjoy going as often as I can to benefit my soul. I also love showing off the seaside to company when they come to visit, as I know they don't get the opportunity to enjoy its benefits very often either.

We're rewarded with pretty shells, flipping rocks to hold crabs of all colors and sizes, sticking our toes in anemones, and holding purple starfish. I squeal as I get squirted by a clam and they laugh at my reaction as they figure I should be used to the squirting fountains by now. Nope, it catches me by surprise every time.

My oldest sister, Lynnette, is filling me in on her patients as a family doctor, and I can't wait to see her reaction when I show her Matt's tanks. My middle sister, Angel, is happily recounting stories of her math students and how excited she is to release the math manual that she's labored over. Mom is just enjoying watching us interact like the good old days and looking out to sea, thinking of dad, who is probably looking down from heaven, happy to see his family all together. I show them the place where the scuffle took place with the fake Daniel, and they look horrified when I recount the details.

Mom exclaims, "Thank God you were protected. I think your angels have been working overtime to protect you these last few weeks."

If they only knew all the times I was in danger. I haven't told them too many details to prevent them from worrying over me.

I head home to toss a salad and cook some basmati rice. We all love working in the kitchen together. We find our rhythm as we set a fancy table with candles, with music softly playing in the background while we banter back and forth.

Mom hears the knock at the door first and hurries to greet Matt with a huge hug, thanking him for the generous plane ride and ushering him in to meet my sisters. He is surrounded by four females, all clamoring for his attention, and he takes it all in stride since he's used to having sisters. I greet him with a chaste kiss and invite everyone to take a seat to partake together.

I invite Matt to say grace, and we'd already planned that he would make his big announcement during the meal. I can tell my family is watching our interactions with interest and sizing him up, weighing whether he is worthy of me. They're protective and want the best for me, which is why their opinion matters to me too. The meal is a culinary success. I can't wait any longer, so I give Matt "the look" that it is time for the unveiling.

Matt clears his throat, and says, "I think it is time you all know that I have been working for years on a very important project and have successfully launched it. I will bring you on a field trip tomorrow to see it for yourselves, so you can understand the impact this will have on Marina and our relationship."

Interestingly, he wants to do a show and tell as he did for me, which I think is a great idea, but I know curiosity will make my family ask a lot of questions. They surprise me by refraining, and we settle back for an evening of getting to hear Matt's testimony and his God journey. Then, we show him our tradition of closing all the lights off in the house, lying down on the floor in the living room with our heads in the middle while praying to God. We pray for each other, our country, Israel, and anything that's on our hearts, and it's a special bonding time of connecting in the spirit. Matt confesses that he has never experienced anything quite like this before but loves the idea of keeping this as a family tradition.

We relax in the hot tub under the stars, enjoying the night sounds and each other's company. Matt has decided to stay the night so he can take us to his lab early in the morning.

I get up early to flip some eggs, toast, and sausages and make some coffee for the road. The weather is perfect with no rain in the forecast and I'm acting like a giddy schoolgirl. Matt comes up behind me for a hug and can't help but laugh at my excitement.

We all squish into my truck, marveling at the views along the way. The ride is spent sharing our miracle stories growing up, like how Lynnette was healed of asthma bronchitis at the age of twelve, and how my parents were both delivered from drinking and smoking when they said "yes" to Jesus. Matt is amazed at the power of God and transformation evidenced in our lives.

We arrive at our destination, and I rush out to give Hulio a hug and introduce him all around. I can't wait to see everyone's reaction to the unveiling that is about to take place. I grab my sisters' arms, pulling them along while Matt escorts mom on his arm to the secret entrance of the underground lab. Their eyes widen with surprise at the lit torches and the path that leads to the chamber filled with tanks.

The questions burst forth, and Hulio raises his hand in silence as he introduces Matt's accomplishment with gusto. Then, Matt explains the science behind the solution, minerals, and soil while elaborating on the light capsules in the States that complete the healing process. Lynnette is flabbergasted at how this works, while Angel is taking it all in with wonder, thinking of all the people who will have hope instead of a death sentence like our father and his four siblings.

Mom is crying softly at witnessing a cancer cure before her very eyes and says, "Now I understand the fight, the scope, and the magnificence of your work and how it will affect the whole world and my daughter." She wipes her eyes and continues, "We have a lot to ponder and take in. I will pray with vigilance for wisdom as to your involvement every step of the way."

The rest of the day is spent enjoying the lake, the amazing lunch prepared by Hulio, and visiting the extraction site by boat of the soil used to generate the formula. It is such an interesting process that it fully captivates Lynnette in learning the intricacies related to the whole process. It wouldn't surprise me at all if she wanted to be involved in helping in some capacity.

We say our heartfelt goodbyes to Hulio and make our way back home, leaving Matt behind for the night to get some more work done while I enjoy my family. This allows us to openly hash out how this will affect my life and our relationship. They produce some good points for me to think through, and the evening is spent praying through the list. They do give their thumbs up of approval of Matteo as a man of unquestionable character, quality, and a good marriage partner, but I question whether I can live with the consequences that come with such a discovery.

The next day, after church, we plan to meet my cousins and Matt at the beach for a picnic and explore some hiking trails. I know of a pretty waterfall with gorgeous views along the way, tall cedars, green ferns, and towering red maples. Bo, Rebecca, and the kids are thrilled to see my whole family together, and hugs are exchanged all around. We set off with the twins teasing Matt and me with kissing noises as we stroll hand in hand, which makes us all giggle and remember being their age.

Matt is acting a little strange and nervous, which I attribute to being around so many family members, or maybe his business has got him wound up. I see him bend down and pick up an old bottle tab shaped like a silver ring and put it in his pocket. Then, it dawns on me that he is gathering up the nerve to propose to me at the waterfall in front of all my family. No wonder he's acting up; this is the big moment. Meanwhile, I have time to prepare myself mentally and pray if he is God's best for me. I put a fleece out there to God, asking for a sign of a rainbow at the falls, as this is the second most important decision of my life. The first is saying "yes" to Jesus and confessing Him as my Savior and Lord of my life.

When I say yes, it means I'm making a lifelong commitment. Divorce is not an option, so I'd better be 100 percent certain that he is the one I want to spend the rest of my life with. There is no going back until death does us part. I know I love him, and he loves me, and when I compare him to any other guy in my life, he wins first place. In my book, there is no other man who can compare to him, so that's a pretty good indicator for my left brain. My right brain is screaming yes at the top of my lungs, so now it's up to what God thinks.

I gasp when I see the waterfall come into view because there is not only one rainbow but double rainbows are gracing us with their beauty. Wow, a double confirmation is exactly what I needed to let my emotions now catch up to my brain. I allow myself to experience this defining moment to the fullest of my childhood dreams. Call me a romantic if you like, but I'm going to soak in every sappy second and I just hope I haven't imagined all this and am not disappointed in the end. My family is busy taking pictures and exclaiming over the two rainbows when Matt approaches me with bright eyes and a big smile.

He gets down on one knee, pulls out the bottle ring, and commences with, "Marina, you dropped into my world and rocked it with love, joy, and passion. I cannot imagine my life without you by my side, completing me. Would you do me the honor of saying yes to becoming my wife, companion, best friend, and confidante? I promise to cherish you for as long as God gives me breath."

I'm relishing the ideal moment as hundreds of thoughts pulse through me. The seconds tick by, causing panic in my beloved's eyes until I passionately declare, "Yes, I will marry you, Matteo Morales! I know God parachuted you into my life for such a time as this and our lives were meant to be entwined for His purposes."

I jump into his waiting arms, and we seal the declaration with a kiss that sets everyone to cheering, clapping, and whooping. We take pictures. Hugs, congratulations, and tears of joy are shed at the momentous occasion my family had the privilege to witness and be a part of.

Mom comes over and holds my face in her hands, and says, "I'm so happy I got to see my baby girl declare her love to her special man. I'm so proud of you and I know your father is also looking down with a big smile from heaven."

My sisters engulf me in excited hugs, and I ask them if they would be my maid of honor and bridesmaids as well as Rebecca, to which they all enthusiastically agree. Next, I ask the twins to be our flower girl and ring bearer, and they're thrilled to be involved. I can't wait to share the good news with Matt's side of the family and set a date. Lots to discuss and plans to make, but in my heart, I'm thanking God for planting a stranger on my doorstep who broke down my defenses and came in like a whirlwind of love.

Who knows what the future holds? I anticipate adventures, challenges, more inventions, mountaintops, and valleys. But as long as God is at the helm and center of it all, it will be a journey to record for the ages and generations to come. Carpe diem, seize the day!

Appendix A

Recipes for Cheesy Chicken Chowder and Glazed Balsamic Chicken

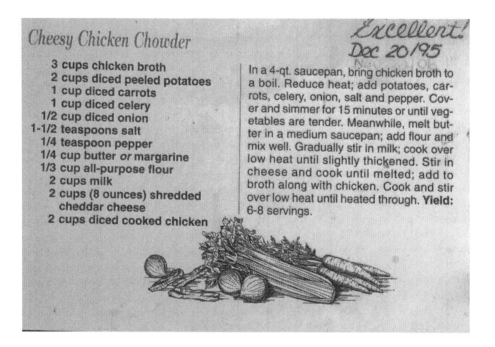

Cheesy Chicken Chowder

Excellent!
Dec 20/95

3 cups chicken broth
2 cups diced peeled potatoes
1 cup diced carrots
1 cup diced celery
1/2 cup diced onion
1-1/2 teaspoons salt
1/4 teaspoon pepper
1/4 cup butter *or* margarine
1/3 cup all-purpose flour
2 cups milk
2 cups (8 ounces) shredded
  cheddar cheese
2 cups diced cooked chicken

In a 4-qt. saucepan, bring chicken broth to a boil. Reduce heat; add potatoes, carrots, celery, onion, salt and pepper. Cover and simmer for 15 minutes or until vegetables are tender. Meanwhile, melt butter in a medium saucepan; add flour and mix well. Gradually stir in milk; cook over low heat until slightly thickened. Stir in cheese and cook until melted; add to broth along with chicken. Cook and stir over low heat until heated through. **Yield:** 6-8 servings.

Glazed Balsamic Chicken

By The Canadian Living Test Kitchen

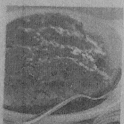

**Glazed Balsamic
Chicken**
Photography by Yvonne
Duivenvoorden

Serving(s)
4

**Yes, have chicken
tonight**

- Chicken Schnitzel
- 20-Minute Chicken
  Goulash
- Island Chicken and Rice
- One-Pot Chicken Pesto
  Pasta
- Hoisin Baked Chicken
- Chicken Lo Mein
- Baked Chicken Tortilla
  Roll-Ups

See all recipe collections

General Category : Main Course
Food Group : Poultry-Chicken
Preparation Method : Skillet

This juicy chicken, with its sweet and sour glaze, from the May 2004 issue of Canadian Living ("Yes, Have Chicken Tonight!") is so simple that you can make it from start to finish in 15 minutes. Serve with mashed potatoes or noodles.

Ingredients

- 1/4 cup (50 mL) all-purpose flour
- 1/4 tsp (1 mL) each salt and pepper
- 4 boneless skinless chicken breasts (about 1-1/2 lb/750 g)
- 2 tbsp (25 mL) extra-virgin olive oil
- 3 cloves garlic, minced
- 1/2 tsp (2 mL) crumbled dried sage or rosemary
- 1 cup (250 mL) chicken stock
- 2 tbsp (25 mL) balsamic vinegar
- 2 tsp (10 mL) liquid honey
- 1 tbsp (15 mL) chopped fresh parsley

Preparation

In shallow dish or plastic bag, combine flour, salt and pepper. Add chicken and turn or shake to coat.

In large nonstick skillet, heat half of the oil over medium heat; fry chicken, turning once, until no longer pink inside, 12 minutes. Remove to plate and keep warm.

Add remaining oil to pan; cook garlic and sage just until golden, about 1 minute. Sprinkle with any remaining flour; cook, stirring, for 30 seconds. Stir in stock, vinegar and honey; cook until thickened enough to coat back of spoon.

Return chicken and any accumulated juices to pan, turning to coat; cook until chicken is glazed, about 1 minute. Sprinkle with parsley.

Nutritional information

Per serving: about 311 cal, 41 g pro, 10 g total fat (2 g sat. fat), 12 g carb, trace fibre, 99 mg chol, 433 mg sodium. % RDI: 2% calcium, 9% iron, 1% vit A, 5% vit C, 7% folate.

Appendix B

My journey: This book originated during Covid on October 10, 2021 where I felt God impressed upon me to write 500 words per day for 90 days. I thrilled to wake up every morning to a blank canvas, ready to write the next adventure, not knowing where it would take me. What a joy, surprise and healing journey it turned out to be!

27542043R00116